Magical Tales

Edgar and the Little Folk

Written and Illustrated

by Anita Friend

Copyright Text © 2014 Anita Friend
Inside illustrations © 2014 Anita Friend
Cover design © 2014 Anita Friend
All rights reserved.

ISBN-13: 978-1502545008

In Memory of

Patrick James Byrne Churcher

And to

Corinne, Kay, Gina and Olivia

Everything billowed and blew
In a turmoil where nothing was new
Save a tempering tome,
Saying - all's ready, all's hoping, all's home,
And I'll tell all, to whoever would choose,
To catch tatters and tips in puddles and pools
In a piggyback place
Today, in the space of a poem.

CONTENTS

The Broomstick	1
The Little Folk	6
After the Storm	51
A Tree	55
Return to the Woods	56
The Great Adventure	60
The "Good" Fairies	125
Sophie and George	134
The Great Adventure Continues	147
Some Wool, a Beetroot & a Hunting Sheep	158
Grimweed, Stark and Walter	166
A Tale of Hope	190
Major Change	199
The Square Heads and Illwilly	221
Sea Mists and High Hopes	227
Edgar Lost and Found	243

The Broomstick

One day in early autumn, two sisters were walking on the Downs when they found a little broomstick lying on the ground.

"What's this?" asked Jodie. "How odd - a

broomstick." She stooped to pick it up. "I wonder what sort of witch owned this." She imagined a small, warty witch hunting round looking for her broomstick.

"Let's see," said Bess. "It's a toy, perhaps?"

Jodie slipped the broomstick in her rucksack.

"This path would have been part of a hill fort in ancient times," Jodie started. "In the olden days, when the Romans came to Britain….."

Her sister interrupted, "I wish the ancients had provided a few benches. Oh look there's a bench," she said pointing down the hill, "there - beneath that crooked tree." Bess turned off the path and Jodie followed.

They sat down on the not-so ancient bench and took in the views before them: the green and yellow fields, the rolling, hazy hills and beyond the hills, the sea.

"This is pleasant," Jodie said, and for a while it was.

Bess opened up her rucksack and pulled out two tin-foil packages.

"They're egg mayonnaise." She handed a package

to her sister. "There was storm damage round here. A few really big trees were blown down. Sad, but then it clears the way for new growth - so they say."

"Who say?" Jodie was gazing down the hill. "Look there's the car park down there. I can see our car. We must have walked all the way around the hill."

There was no more conversation as they finished their sandwiches.

Bess brushed crumbs from her jeans and turned towards her sister. "We should be heading home."

They gathered their belongings and stood up, and as they did so, a large crow, that had been perched all the while on a branch above, ruffled his wings, hopped and flew up through the tree. He gave a shrill and mournful cry as he rose into a darkening sky.

Bess shivered. She buttoned up her jacket. "Is it me or is it getting chilly?"

They pocketed the tin foil wrappers, shuffled on their rucksacks and set off down the hill towards the car park.

Much later, back at home, Jodie unpacked her

rucksack and took out the broomstick. She was sitting in her bedroom by the window and now she held the broomstick to the light and studied it awhile. It was clearly a well-made little object, slightly battered and several tiny feathers were stuck between the twigs. She popped the broomstick in a small china jug that was standing on the windowsill.

"Yes, very curious." Jodie yawned, then rose stiffly from the chair, slumped down upon her bed, rolled over and soon was fast asleep.

All was quiet in the room - just a ticking clock - hardly a sound. All was peaceful. But now - not so for Jodie - for within her sleep she was dreaming of strange things - strange goings on - in ancient woods, on rolling hills - of crows, bees, butterflies, and honey pots. She saw skies of pinks and purple like sunrise and sunset in quick succession. She heard chiming bells and strange music. Now she saw a little witch. Now a very old man whose name was…. was….yes she caught his name… "Edgar McNezzar."

Jodie woke with a start. Bess was at the door.

"Did I wake you? I thought you might like a cup of tea. I've put the kettle on."

"Yes, that would be nice. I had such a strange dream," she told her sister.

Over the next few nights Jodie continued to have strange dreams, but then even stranger things began to happen, for soon, so it seemed, all the creatures of the wood were moving in - that is - moving into her bedroom. She would wake early in the morning and find a bird flying round the room, a toad sitting on the windowsill, a line of green, leggy insects climbing up the wall. Then there were the ants, the snails, and worst of all, the mice.

"I don't know how they're getting in. It's all too much, it really is. It's almost as if those little creatures feel that this is their home and I can tell you - things are getting worse. Last night I woke and had to chase a squirrel out. It really is too much."

The Little Folk

Estine raced past Elzamere the elf and flew towards the crooked tree.

"Estine!" the elf called out.

"Can't stop," Estine flashed her dark eyes and in a swirl of greens and white, she was gone.

"She can't stop! Why can't she stop?"

Estine flew up and landed on a branch. "I'm here."

"Right," said Roly Poly. He was speaking to a small group of fairies. He flicked his flop of fair hair and grinned. "Follow me. Close your wings, then arms forward, ankles bent." He looked round, stepped forward off the branch, dropped straight down and landed neatly on a flower beneath. The flower stem dipped, sprung back and sent him bouncing from one flower to another.

The fairy Dominic was next. He crouched down and bounded off the branch. He made a perfect landing, and a perfect bounce. He was up and off, and the other fairies, Estine, Cora, Poppy, Bella, Little Ivy and Piper followed too, one by one, with a perfect drop and bounce.

Elzamere watched them disappear from sight. "They're up to no good," she muttered to herself. But the fairies were just having fun, and soon, they were swinging on the threads of an old abandoned spider's web, chasing dragonflies or like little Ivy, merely following a creeping, freckled bug.

Elzamere returned to her room in the hollow trunk of the oak. She took off her outdoor jacket and smoothed down her wrinkled leaf green skirt. (She had a fondness for wearing green, brown and russet colours). Elzamere pulled off her boots and stomped over to a storage chest. "And I've so much to do," she said in conversation with herself. She fiddled with the sharpened twig that held her long dark hair coiled up and twisted in a bun. "It will soon be autumn and there's pickling, potting and sewing to be doing, and who will make the winter mats? Me - I get no help."

Elzamere swung open the lid of the wooden storage chest and took out a sewing basket. She lit a waxy twig for extra light and stuck it in a pot. Then she found her tiny spectacles, placed them on her neat and tiny nose and sat down.

"I wonder what Edgar would think of their behaviour?"

She snapped open the basket lid, found some thistle-cotton thread, and quite deftly, threaded up a needle.

Edgar McNezzar had been busy in the cellar of the oak. He was a clever gnome who could make things out of wood and metal - skills learned long ago. His old friend Jasper Sprig and his band, The Travelling Bow-Kneed Band, would be arriving any day. The trumpets, trombones, saxophones and even the guitars were too heavy for this older group, so these musical instruments had been fitted with little wheels. Edgar had taken on the task to make new wheels to replace the old, and now they were ready.

"A job well done," he thought with satisfaction.

At noon, Edgar left the cellar and climbed the tree. He found a sunny spot near the top, sat down and soon was drifting off to sleep. Now in his dozing dream he heard the rustling leaves like muffled whispered words. They seemed to grow more urgent as he drifted deeper into sleep. Then suddenly he heard a clear and haunting voice:

"Edgar McNezzar he is calling us, calling us. He is calling us."

"What's that?" Edgar felt a shift, a loss of certainty, a falling. He woke startled from his dream. He was on the same oak, beneath the same bright sky, but within himself, he felt the tremor of his dream.

Later that day Elzamere decided to visit her friends, Bead and Silk. They lived on the second floor, No. 3, The Old Beech Tree.

"They will offer tea and sympathy," she thought, and they did.

"I can't take much more," Elzamere complained. She took another sip of mint tea. "Those fairies - all they ever do is play. Nobody understands how sensitive I am, - apart from you of course." She blinked her moss green eyes as if tears might fall, and turned towards her friend.

"Yes I know, poor Elzamere." Bead was casting long loops of gossamer thread onto heavy, wooden knitting needles. "I say, put your foot down. You can't have fairies flying all over you."

She turned to her husband. "What do you think Silk?"

"Hmm," he responded.

Rondal Silkwood, her husband, was seated on a mushroom. It was tipped back against the wall. He was reading a large book and humming through his fingers. His woolly, homemade clothes overlapped in rolls about his bony frame and his socks dangled loosely from his toes.

"Yes," Bead continued, "you should put a stop to all that childish play." She placed her knitting down. "Have some more tea Elzamere? Do take a wrinkle-pip pie. I remember when fairies were far less trouble. Now...." Bead patted her smooth, red hair and tilted her head towards her friend, "I've heard they go into the homes of the big folk and steal from peanut butter pots. Isn't that right Silk?"

Silk misheard, "No thanks love, but I will have a wrinkle-pip pie." He tipped his mushroom upright, placed his book down on the table and popped a pie into his mouth.

Bead changed the subject. "We have been sorting out some of the books to sell at the market tomorrow. We have far too many, as you can see," she gestured round the room. "They all but cover up the windows and I'm forever tripping over them. Will you be going to the market tomorrow?"

"Yes Bead."

"Fine, we can we can go together."

Trading took place within the Gateway Trees that circled a hill to the North of the ancient oak. This hill had its own magic protection and when the big folk came anywhere near the Gateway Trees, they would suddenly be seized by a certainty that they had far more important things to do than wander about a hillside.

Elzamere, Bead and Silk arrived early at the market. There was the usual air of hustle and bustle with little folk rolling barrels, pushing wheelbarrows, arranging displays or simply looking for somewhere to place their baskets on the ground. Signs had been erected:- "Nuts, Fruit and Pickles" "Ales Brewed by Local Gnomes" and these local gnomes, standing just beneath the signs, were smiling broadly, chatting and clearly hoping for a good day's trade.

Elzamere and Bead set down their baskets on the grass amongst the other traders. Elzamere had brought some herbs in green, pink and purple bags, labelled mint, rosemary, chives, thyme, and so on, while Bead was hoping to sell some homemade clothes: knitted socks, gloves and matching hats, and Silk had brought a wheelbarrow full of books to sell.

Very soon a small group of little folk were milling round and business proceeded:-

"Any of these in a smaller size?" a tiny pixie asked.

"Do you have any soft-leaf quilted hoods?"

"How much are the bags of rosemary?"

"Have you any books by Percy Lard?"

And so it went on. In a quieter moment, Bead gazed about.

"Oh look there's Edgar, just across the way with a barrel of his...." - she squinted at a sign, "Mellow Brew."

Silk glanced up. "I'll just pop over and say hello." He left his wheelbarrow full of books and wandered off.

Edgar was sitting on a stool beside his barrel. He looked up when Silk approached. "Try my homebrew young man. And how are things with you?"

"Not bad. And how are you? - I see you have your helpers."

Roly Poly beamed and Bella dipped an acorn cup into the brew to nearly overflowing and handed it to Silk.

"Yes," replied Edgar "and the others are here - somewhere."

Not far off Poppy was standing by a toadstool listening to a bright-eyed little pixie. "I have glitter stones, barley beads, shells and dangling knotted string…." said the pixie.

Estine and Ivy were listening to an elf. "These are top quality humming stones. They have perfect pitch." She placed green, pink, blue, and yellow stones in a circle on a grass. "Listen - …." - "HummMMMMMumm"

"Do they make these sounds underwater?" asked a gentleman with bulging, froglike eyes.

"Yes they certainly do."

"Very nice," he hesitated. "Have you any wind chimes?"

Piper was watching a goblin.

"Here we have coils, tins and springs, all clean and polished," said the goblin.

"Where did you get them? Did they come from a roadside skip?"

"No. I brought them in from a recycling tip."

Dominic and Cora were staring at a sign: "Perception Spectacles for Sale"

A large pot bellied gnome appeared. "Try these on, son."

Dominic replied, "I don't need glasses. I can see perfectly - just like a bird. If I fly right up to that cloud I can look down and see a mouse cleaning its whiskers."

Cora agreed. "He can fly as high as a cloud. Once he nearly collided with a plane."

"Well you might see whiskers on a mouse, but obviously you don't see the planes too well. Perhaps you do need glasses, but wait, these are no ordinary spectacles," and he handed Dominic a pair of horn-rimmed glasses. "These are Rhinoceros Spectacles. Try them on."

Dominic placed them on his nose. He saw nothing but a blurry image, and then suddenly he felt strong, safe, and free from any danger. It was as if he wore armour like a knight, or the padding of a rhinoceros. "I feel great," he said, but then he took a step forward and tripped.

"No," said the gnome. "No, no you can't expect to walk with them on. You wear them as a pick-you-up, a tonic, something to make you feel better. Come try some more - both of you."

Dominic handed back the Rhinoceros glasses and tried a pair of yellow, parrot glasses, and soon he was laughing.

Cora chose some jade green, cat's eyes specs. She made a funny face. "Do I have whiskers and a tail? I feel like purring," and she too started laughing.

Now Bead, back across the way, had spotted them. The elf raised an eyebrow and elbowed Elzamere, as much to say - "Fairies making fools of themselves in front of everyone."

"Well," continued the gnome, "are you interested in these special spectacles? Do you have money, or something to exchange?"

"We have our songs."

"Sorry. No songs today."

The day passed pleasantly enough. Elzamere and Bead had sold their goods and found the time to do some shopping.

"We did well," said Bead, "but …where is Silk? I bet he's buying more books."

"No he is speaking to that gnome over there."

"… and will they help me to read in the dark?" Silk's eyes widened. He was staring blindly through a small pair of Mole glasses.

"Certainly," replied the gnome.

Silk returned empty handed. "I thought I might buy some mole glasses," he explained, "but when I put them on - I couldn't see a thing. Still my sense of smell improved."

A goblin was poking round the wheelbarrow. "What's this? 'Learn to Speak Trog in 30 Days' - but surely there are only 10 words in their language and three of them are swear words."

"No, no, no, you underestimate the trog. They are far more expressive than that."

"Grunt, grunt I think," said the goblin dismissively. "Not for me," and he walked away.

"Some goblins…!" Bead exclaimed. "Come on Silk. Let's go home." She turned to Elzamere. "I bought some thistle thread and a polished nutshell tub. What have you bought? - Ah bramble jam and … so many feather dusters. I hope the jam is for you and the dusters for the fairies."

Next day Elzamere stood with her back to the twisting roots that hid the little door of the oak. She scowled at the fairies.

"All is not well. I've seen you bouncing from

flower to flower like fat little bees, chasing moths, dragonflies, other whatnots and generally swinging about on old spider webs. Are you listening to me?"

Little Ivy was dancing in the air, Roly Poly pulled a funny face and Bella giggled. Elzamere was furious. She turned and strode back inside the tree and slammed the door shut.

"Edgar!" her shrill voice echoed through the hollow of the tree. She stomped up the creaky, spiral staircase that wound around the inside of the trunk until it opened out at the first line of branches. Then Elzamere climbed crisscross quickly up the tree. She found Edgar snoozing in the sun.

"They don't take any notice of me."

Edgar woke suddenly. Elzamere was blazing forth. "I'm at my wits' end. I spend all my time mopping up after rats, bats, moles, tripping up over acorns, leaves, and rabbit droppings. Those fairies - they're no help. I don't think they ever do a single thing of use."

"That's just not so," said Edgar. "That's not so at all. Poppy sings and make up songs."

Elzamere crossed and uncrossed her arms.

"Piper whistles like the birds. Estine practices her knots - that is learning to untie knots - a very useful skill."

Elzamere shifted on her feet and was rocking back and forth.

"Cora knows the stories of the woods. Roly Poly makes up games. Ivy's very fond of lady birds."

"Ivy -" Elzamere's eyes blazed, "that one. Can she hear? Can she speak? I'm sure she's not all there."

"That's not kind," said Edgar.

Elzamere sniffed and still rocking back and forth upon her feet, the pointed toes of her tiny shoes were curling up.

Edgar continued: "Dominic is strong and fearless."

"That's no use to me - none of it." Elzamere turned abruptly and stomped away.

But she was not one to give up easily and once again, she stood before the fairies. "Listen," she said fiercely, "I'm taking no nonsense. Now if anyone is without a feather-duster …."

They all had their feather-dusters ready. They

waved them in the air, and then fell into a roll-about, feather-duster brawl.

"Stop that," Elzamere snapped at them. "Now - there, there and there - dust, stack and polish," and she left them to it.

The fairies set to dusting, stacking, polishing, but before the day was out - they rebelled.

"It's too much." Cora threw the duster in the air.

"Enough," said Roly Poly. He flicked back his flop of hair, and threw his duster down.

"Enough," said Poppy.

"Enough," said Dominic and the others too, threw their dusters on the ground.

"Now…," said Roly Poly, the others crowded round, "we'll have some fun, and Cowpatti" (his new name for Elzamere) "will pay. This is what we'll do…"

That evening Elzamere left the oak. She was wearing her heavy walking shoes and was carrying a pointed stick. Clearly, she was off collecting roots. The fairies sneaked into her room carrying piles of cobwebs and a pot of honey. The cobwebs were scattered on the floor. Then Roly Poly found Elzamere's soft leaf slippers lying on the floor by the door, and filled them up with honey.

Later the elf returned. As she entered she placed a pile of roots in a big pot beside the door, took off her muddy shoes and in the dimness of the room, slipped into her slippers. But now what was this? A squelching mess was oozing through her toes. She snatched the slippers, the left, the right, flung them on the floor and in a blind rage, with sticky feet and hopping mad, she dashed about the room. Too late - the cobwebs had gathered to her feet like candy floss.

Elzamere raced up the spiral staircase. "Edgar!" Edgar was sitting on a branch. He had one eye closed and was studying the bright full moon.

Elzamere dumbly pointed to her fluffy feet and sobbed, "Err…? Err…? hmm…?"

"Elzamere," he said, "go and see the little ones. They are dancing on the grassy ridge. My old friend Jasper Sprig is here and The Travelling Bow-Kneed Band are playing once again. We will all be there, come have some fun."

"What about my feet?"

Instead of looking down, he looked up at the moon. "You know," he said, "up there on the moon is the Sea of Tranquility."

"Well go sit in it," she snapped and off she stormed.

Returning to her room, she sat down. "If he won't help me I'll sort them out myself." And Elzamere devised a plan.

Up on the hill the music of Travelling Bow-Kneed Band filled the air. There had been wiz-ding jazzy tunes like "The Caterpillar Trot" and softer melodies: "Dark is the Dimple Weed". The fairies loved to dance, and as they danced, the night air sparkled from the brilliance of their wings, with greens, blues, turquoise, mauves and cream-pink coral colours.

Now Jasper Sprig, the leader of the band, was singing a soulful song:

"I'm a roaming kind of gnome,
I travelled East, I've travelled West,
I've hiked the mountain, scaled the crest,
And though this land of yours,
Is mellow, green and yellow,

*Perhaps you'll understand I cannot stay,
I'm moving on, moving on.*

*Yes, I'm a roaming, rustic sort of gnome,
Not a 'put your feet up' kind of fellow,
My freedom is my garden, my city and my home
And though this land of yours,
Is mellow, green and yellow,
Perhaps you'll understand I cannot stay
I'll be moving on, moving on.*

*I've walked the high road and the low,
I've seen the seasons come and go,
I've seen the ebb, I've seen the flow.
So can you understand?
I know this land is mellow, green and yellow,
But I am moving on, moving on."*

The full moon cast its light upon scene, but in the deeper shadows, there were passers-by: a hedgehog snuffling in the undergrowth; a fox who was there and then was gone; a barn owl; a mouse…..

The music played on. Cora was dramatic in her dance. She wore black and silver and tonight her hair was spiky pink. Dominic had a stomping style. He wore grey and silver. Poppy swirled in red and pinks with tiny sparkles like stars in the darkness of her hair. Bella leaped. She like blues and greens and tonight she wore silver seeds threaded neatly through her orange plait. Estine twirled in green and cream and frothy white. Her long, dark hair was loose and free. Roly Poly was a rocker and a roller. His suit was coffee cream with the name 'Elvis' embroidered on his shirt. Ivy always wore white with a sash of ivy that crossed over and fell from her shoulder to her waist. Her shoulder-length, fair hair was plain and loose. She flittered and watched the glitter patterns in the air - and little Piper he wore a sage coloured suit with a dark green tie and big collar. He watched the band.

"Hey fairy butterfly," Jasper sang
"Hey fairy butterfly,
Sing my song, sing my song,
I'm a bee without a sting.

Sing my song, yea, sing my song.
You're a queen without a king.
Sing my song,
I've a heart without a home,
You've a crown without a throne.
You're a fairy, I'm a gnome.
Be my queen.
Yea, Yea. Sing my song, sing my song,
Sing my song.
Yea, Yea. Sing my song, sing my song,
Sing my song."

Now Jasper addressed the audience. "I wrote this next song - *The Melancholy Blues* - when I was going through a bad patch.

Sometimes it's tough, it's tough.
It's the short straw that we choose,
But no, it ain't so bad, it ain't so bad
As the melancholy blues.

A goblin stole my coat, he stole my hat,
Then ran off in my shoes.
But no, it ain't so bad, it ain't so bad
As the melancholy blues.

I was buried in the snow
One foot deep I know, freezing, sneezing,
But no, it ain't so bad, it ain't so bad
As the melancholy blues.

My fishing line was taut,
A mighty fish was caught.
He flashed his fin, then hauled me in.
But hey, it ain't so bad, it ain't so bad,
As the melancholy blues.

I was threatened by a frog
'If we fight,' he said 'you'll lose.'
- I fought and lost.
But man, it ain't so bad, no, it ain't so bad
As the melancholy blues.

Take it away Pixie, Lefty on the drums." Jasper pulled out a large handkerchief, mopped his glowing brow and stuffed the handkerchief back into his pocket. Then he glanced slowly about the audience and raised his arms.

"Do you want to hear the tale of the Web Foot Buccaneer?"

"Tell us," cried the fairies.

With just the rhythm of the drums, he began:

"Beneath the Northern Dipdown Hills are pools and water spills,
Where a paddle boat or raft, or shoe canoe, or other craft
Can take you to the sea.
But on your way take care
For somewhere in the willow weeds,
Where the ducks, the drakes, the canny coots,
The water snakes
And puffy pillow swans all gather,
There is a wild and angry goose - a buccaneer,
Ever waiting, ever watching, ever near -
So be aware - if you take a boat or shoe canoe -
This wily wader, this space invader -
Might be after you.

Tripper don't be a dipper for the day.
Tripper don't be a dipper for the day."

(Speeding up)

"Tripper don't be a dipper for the day."

(Faster, louder)

The fairies were whizzing around, dancing.

"Tripper don't be
Tripper don't be
Tripper don't be
Don't be - Don't be - Don't be
A dipper for the day.
Tripper don't be
Don't be - Don't be - Don't be
A dipper for the day.
Tripper don't be
Tripper don't be
Tripper don't be
Don't be - Don't be - Don't be
A dipper for the day.
Tripper don't be
Don't be - Don't be - Don't be
a dipper for the day."

Then - a rapid roll of drums - a clash of symbols that faded slowly to a hush and all was quiet. The bandsmen would have bowed, but being very old and somewhat bent already, they merely nodded at the fairies - and the fairies, beaming all the colours of the rainbow flew up, clapped and cheered.

Once again, the bandsmen nodded. Then they rolled their instruments aside, refilled their acorn cups with brew and sat down to take a break.

Jasper leaned over to Edgar. "My old mate, you're living quietly now. Remember the good old days - the great adventures we once had. We miss you - the gang is still around. Come visit us sometime."

"I'm getting old. My memory's not so good."

"Our memories have been worse and better - but there's still life in us old gnomes - what you say?"

"Yes may be," said Edgar mildly.

After a little while, Piper stepped forward to speak to the singer of the band. "Mr Jasper Sprig…," he began, "Mr Jasper Sprig may I… join your band?"

"You too?" said Jasper Sprig looking up. "Roly Poly was telling me he plays air guitar. How old are you? You know you have to be at least 103 to join our band."

"I'm six," said Piper.

"Well one day may be."

"I've got my own tin whistle and I practise all the time."

"Ask me again in 20 years."

"Is that a very long time?"

"No - no time at all."

Then Jasper Sprig took a sip of cider mint and looked about. "Where's Elzamere my favourite little elf."

Roly Poly looked guilty. "She's having a trouble with her feet."

"What a shame. No dancing for Elzamere tonight."

Elzamere stepped through the door that led down to the cellar of the tree. She carried a spade and sack in one hand and a lighted candle in the other. The muddy passage followed round a twisting tree root and Elzamere descended cautiously. The air was stale and musty and in the dull light she found herself stepping over creepy things like the skeletons of mice.

"I know it's down here," she said grimly to herself.

"What's down here?" a booming throaty voice echoed through the passageway.

"Who's there?" called Elzamere.

"Who wants to know?"

"Oh it's a mole. Only moles answer every question with a question."

"I'm looking for the gold dust pot. It belongs to the fairy folk and I believe it's in the cellar. I want a little - for the fairies," she said, scrunching up the sack.

"Do you mind if I pass?"

"What pot? What fairies?"

"Excuse me." Elzamere squeezed by the mole.

Eventually the ground levelled out and the passage curved around and led on to a long low-ceilinged room. In the dim light, she could just make out a faint line of iron brackets fixed against a wall. Each bracket held a candle. She lit the first, then walked on and lit another. The room was clear on one side. On the other side, there were boxes, barrels, wooden bins, brass-stoppered pots, and more…

"No not there, or there. More clutter. A maze of clutter, so it seems," she muttered to herself.

There were cutting tools hung in loops of twine against the wall; mighty hammers standing upright in a row; sieves; bellows; cooking pots; more boxes and more brass stoppered pots.

Elzamere continued through the room and then she stopped before a wooden table. It was narrow and tapering like a tree branch - "Edgar's workbench," Elzamere supposed.

She noticed several clay pots stuffed with rolls of paper, writing quills, compasses, rulers and other drawing instruments.

"So this is where Edgar spends his time, and what is this?" A tin barrel with a peeling paper wrapper stated "Baked Beans". Elzamere peered over the rim and dipped her finger in. "It's only candle wax." She sniffed. "All this storage stuff - so where's the gold dust pot?"

A little further on Elzamere came face to face with a standing mirror. It was dark and dusty and threw back a strange, distorted image - a little elf who was plainly grim and stubborn.

"It's nothing like me. I'm much nicer than that," and disregarding the words engraved upon the frame: ***"THIS MIRROR NEVER LIES!"*** Elzamere moved on. Beyond the mirror was a clock. Its dark wood, polished face was carved with woodland flowers, fruits and berries, and the words - *"Summer"* - *"Autumn"* - *"Winter"* - *"Spring"*. The single hand had moved beyond the high point of *"Summer"*.

"Well at least that's working."

At last, she found what she was looking for. Set against the far wall was a large, ancient-looking pot, and holding up her candle, she read the dust encrusted words that ran round the belly of the pot - *"The Rainbow Pot"*. Elzamere dropped the shovel, budged off the pot lid and peered inside. It was full of gold dust.

"I knew it - at last." She placed the candle down, shook the sack and laid it open on the ground. Then she toiled away for several minutes, straining to shovel out the dust and heap it in the sack. Now and then, Elzamere stopped to lift the sack and shuffle it about. Finally she puffed, "Enough is enough."

The sack was just a quarter full, but this was as much as the elf could carry. She let the shovel drop, replaced the lid back on the pot and gathered up the sack. Then awkwardly, carrying her lighted candle in one hand and dragging the heavy load behind her, she retraced her steps back along the room and up the tunnel. Sometime later, a red-faced Elzamere emerged at ground level. Then she heaved and shuffled over to her room and closed the door.

High on the hill ridge the Travelling Bow-Kneed Band played on.

The fairies danced in the old traditional way. To the left - skip, twirl, fly. To the right - skip, twirl, fly. They danced on until the rising of the morning mists, then one by one they drifted home, found a leafy bed and fell asleep.

Next day only the birds and Elzamere woke at dawn - but by mid morning, all the fairies (except Little Ivy) were gathered by the oak. They should have stayed in bed, but Elzamere, had called them in her ear piercing voice, and barely awake and bleary eyed, they had rolled out of bed and shuffled down.

Now here was Elzamere at the foot of the tree, standing between two pots. In one hand she held a brush made from rat's hair.

"Line up now. I want to spruce up your wings."

Elzamere dipped the brush into a pot of snail slime paste, wiped the excess on the pot rim, and then walking round behind the fairies, she slapped the lumpy goo across their wings. Reaching the end, she turned about and walked back up the line. Then she replaced the brush in the snail slime pot and moved over to the other pot. With a trowel she gathered up a heap of gold dust, and working quickly back and forth, plastered gold dust thickly on the fairies wings. The gold-dust stuck - it stuck like heavy gilt.

"Beautiful," she said beaming.

"It's too heavy." Cora was falling backwards.

"But we are grounded," cried Estine.

"I can't move." Bella had folded on her knees.

Even Roly Poly and Dominic could barely move.

"Rubbish. Cora why are you blabbing? Don't you know that all the big folk are wearing gold? It might slow you down a bit to start with, but just now you are weak and spoilt that's all. Really, I go to all this trouble to make you perfect and this is the thanks I get."

Ivy, who had stayed in bed, suddenly shot out. The little fairy had selective hearing - meaning she could only hear some things. She had not heard Elzamere screech that morning, though it had been enough to knock the crow off his perch and set the squirrels all a jitter, but now, quite plainly, little Ivy could hear that somebody was crying. She looked about, up and down the tree, and once again heard crying. It was coming from below. Ivy flew quickly down the tree, down to the ground, and there, she saw Elzamere was strutting up and down giving some kind of lecture while the fairies were staggering about. Ivy was horrified. She flew over to Elzamere, circled round her head, grabbed the sharpened twig that held the elf's hair neatly in a knot and tugged at it. Out it came and Elzamere's long hair tumbled down and fell across her face. Clawing blindly at the air, Elzamere screeched.

"I'll teach you!"

Now Ivy flew fiercely about and swishing the sharp pointed twig like a sword, she jabbed the elf in the elbow several times - at speed. Elzamere screamed and started snatching at the air.

"You little midge, you horrible mosquito. You, you nothing! Just you wait - you'll be sorry."

She was in a rage. But now Ivy was in a rage. In fact, she was in a dazzling rage - her wings flamed pink and scarlet.

"Ivy," called Dominic, "go find Edgar."

"You'll be lucky," Elzamere declared, "He's probably sitting on the moon."

"Ivy," called the fairies, "find Edgar."

"And what will he do?" snapped Elzamere, "Drop off to sleep - snore his disapproval?"

Ivy flew back up the tree and searched about the branches.

"Where is Edgar McNezzar?" she thought. Then in a whisper - "Where is Edgar McNezzar?"

Two squirrels chirruped, a mouse scurried by, insects buzzed, and birds sang.

"Where is Edgar McNezzar?" she said again. "Does anybody know?"- And more loudly - "DOES ANYBODY KNOW?"

"DOES ANYBODY KNOW?" a voice came back like an echo from above. Ivy looked up. A large, black crow with sleek and glossy feathers was standing on the branch above. The crow flapped his wings, then hopped a branch, and moved over to the fairy. Ivy took a step back. She noticed that the crow's eyes were keen and curious and his beak looked very sharp. The crow moved closer and took a sideward glance. Ivy still had the hairpin stick and now she clutched it tightly in her fist.

The crow blinked. "Is that a sword I see before me or a dragon's tooth?" He spoke loud and clear, but there was no meanness in his voice.

Ivy lowered the stick. "It's Elzamere's hair-pin. She has done something to the fairies - they cannot fly. I must find Edgar McNezzar. Have you seen him?"

"Have I seen him? Have I seen him?" He ruffled his wings, hopped about a bit, and then staring upwards to the sky, he squawked, "Let's take a look. Hop on my back," and she did.

The crow spread his wings, flapped and rose into the air. One circle round the oak, up again and off he flew towards the fields. Little Ivy held on tight. The wind raced against her face and wings.

"This is fast," Ivy thought. Then leaning to one side, she scanned the land below. The crow, with his keen black eyes was searching in the distance. He could see beyond the trees, beyond the hills and yet further to the sea.

"He can't be that far away," Ivy thought. "Look below - there is Jasper and his band moving through the woods. Let me ask them what they know."

Jasper spotted the black crow swooping fast towards them. The crow landed with a skipping hop and Ivy, unused to flying by crow, rolled forward and tumbled to the ground.

"What's all the hurry?" asked Jasper.

Ivy straightened up, flapped her crumpled wings and caught her breath.

"Do you know where Edgar is?"

"Yea, well yea. Let me think. Last night we had a drink I told him I was leaving early in the morning - we've got a gig in the West Country. I asked him to join us, but he said he had things to do. What's happened to Edgar - he's become a real old stick in the mud?" Jasper seemed to be thinking of other things, then after a moment, he continued. "I think he said he had some work in his cellar, but I thought he meant late morning, after a long lie in."

"Thanks Jasper." Ivy climbed back on the crow.

"No problem," called Jasper.

She waved goodbye. The crow flapped his

brilliant gloss-black wings and rose into the air. With a loud squawking cry, he flew back towards the hills. Once around the oak and he landed on a branch. This time Ivy rolled sideways off his back. Her face was flushed, her hair tangled from the hurly burly of flying at speed, but she was up at once and set to find Edgar.

"Wait. Don't forget your dragon's tooth."

She gripped the stick. "Thanks."

Then in a flash, she flew through the branches of the tree, down the spiral staircase of the trunk to the cellar door, which stood ajar. Ivy slipped through into the dark, descending passageway. The sparkle from her wings gave light enough to see and she followed down the muddy passageway as it wound around the tree root. Ivy had no fear as she flew through musty air above crumbling, cobwebbed bones. She would find Edgar McNezzar and he would help the fairies. Then she turned another corner and suddenly she stopped. She could go no further. A mole, a big mole was blocking up the passageway. Curled up with his head cupped in one of his large, shovel-like front paws, he was fast asleep. Ivy had come all this way and now she stood firm.

"May I pass? Excuse me, may I pass?"

The mole shifted in his sleep; his nose twitched and he muttered to himself: "Worms - who do they think they are?"

"I'm not a worm." She remembered Elzamere's words, "and I'm not a gnat, or a mosquito, or a nothing. LET ME PASS!" She yelled and held her sword up high. (Or was it a dragon's tooth?)

Suddenly the mole was wide-awake. "Who goes there? What are you? What's your business?"

"I'm Ivy the fairy, and I must speak with Edgar McNezzar. I was told I might find him in the cellar of the tree and we need his help urgently. There's a great deal of trouble up above."

The mole wrinkled up his face. "Who needs trouble?" He curled his toes and rolled over to one side.

Ivy squeezed by the mole and flew on down the tunnel. At last, she reached the point where it levelled out and led to the long, low-ceiling cellar room. Ivy hurried through, passed the wooden bins, the barrels, pots, passed the workbench, and so on. As she came upon the tall standing mirror it glowed with swirling mists of pinks and blues and the bright reflection of a little fairy. She moved beyond the mirror and beyond the clock of seasons, and at last, at the cellar end, found Edgar. The old man was peering into a large, ancient looking pot. Beside the pot, Elzamere's shovel was still lying on the ground.

"Edgar," Ivy began, "Elzamere has…"

Edgar looked up surprised. "Elzamere has…" he continued "been up to mischief."

Edgar McNezzar stood on the top-most branch of the oak, facing south. He slowly raised his arms, drew a deep breath and called:

"Softly, softly send the winds.
Softly, softly breeze.
Test the trees, lift the leaves
And call the winds to me."

He repeated this chant several times. Then suddenly a fierce wind rose and the leaves trembled and shook and the old tree rocked, and way down below at the foot of the tree Elzamere's pots were overturned and the poor little fairies tumbled about in the wind, but the gold dust blew away with the wind, and their wings were free.

"Now softly, softly winds depart," chanted Edgar, and the winds were gone. Edgar gazed up. He studied the sky and looked a little puzzled.

"Ermm, the winds were rather too fierce that time," and he scratched his woolly beard.

Next day Elzamere was fuming. She sat on a tuft of grass drumming her fingers.

"No one respects me. They have gone back to sitting under toadstools and chasing dragonflies. If only I could fly. It's not fair."

"What's not fair?" asked the crow who had overheard Elzamere talking to herself.

"If only I could fly. How do you do it?"

"I have wings. I have feathers. Do you have wings? No. Do you have feathers? No."

The crow was pecking at the ground.

"What are you looking for?" asked Elzamere.

"This and that. This and that. In the days

before…." He drifted, "there were witches. They could fly on broomsticks."

Elzamere looked doubtful. "No, witches are just myths I think."

"Yes and no. Yes and no. Ask Edgar he knows."

"I don't understand anything he says. He talks in riddles and he never listens to me. Anyway, how can a broomstick fly?"

"Stick feathers in a broom, catch the wind and see."

Elzamere sat thinking for some time, and then she sought out Edgar.

"Edgar, will you make me a broomstick? A broomstick that might fly - perhaps?"

"Are you planning to be a witch?"

"May be, then people might listen to me."

"Well I will make you a new broomstick, but I don't think it will fly."

A few days later Edgar presented Elzamere with a new broomstick made from the fine new roots of the oak tree. "It will serve you well," he said.

"Thank you Edgar."

Quickly she returned to her room and spent the afternoon gluing tiny feathers to the broom. "Not bad," she noted. Then she wiped her hands, adjusted her new hairclip, (it was inclined to slip), picked up her newly feathered broomstick and went outside.

No one was about. Elzamere climbed onto the broomstick and waited and waited. Now she licked a finger and held it to the air. There was no wind.

"No wind," she said aloud.

"Try jumping off the cliff." The crow was peering down from an overhanging branch.

Elzamere looked up. "Oh thanks very much," she said peevishly.

"You might just catch the wind," he explained.

"No… I think I will jump from the top of that bush."

So Elzamere dragged the broomstick up through the bush to the peak. She climbed aboard, took a deep breath and jumped. Well it worked. She was airborne and flying through the trees.

"I'll show them," she thought.

But in truth, it was more like a shuttlecock than a flying broomstick. As the wind gathered and changed direction, she went into a spin, up and down, through bushes, brambles, catching twigs, leaves, thistles and spider webs. Suddenly a gust of wind lifted her high into the air, and just as suddenly, it ceased. The 'witch' hovered - turned - and fell back down to earth and the little broomstick stuck, dart like, headfirst in a puddle (of course). Slowly Elzamere emerged. She was muddy and bedraggled.

There was silence in the wood - no creature stirred, and Elzamere stood stock-still with only her moss green eyes, in her mud packed face, moving from left to right, right to left. Then in an instant, she heard them. Somewhere hidden from view they were laughing at her - those wicked fairies. And her blood boiled. She pulled the broomstick from the mud, swung it about her head and crashed it hard against the bushes, the trees and the grasses, and the blows caught several poor fairies.

Dominic and Roly Poly lost no time and flew off to find Edgar McNezzar.

"Quick," they said. "Call the winds. Call the winds. Elzamere is screeching like a demented cat and hitting out at everyone."

"No, it's too soon. I can't call them again so soon," thought Edgar, but when he saw Elzamere thrashing about in her fury, he hurriedly climbed the tree and at the very top, facing north this time, he raised his arms and called:

"Call the winds, call the winds.
Call the winds, call the winds.
Test the trees, lift the leaves
and call the winds to me."

Louder still, and staring upwards at the sky:

"Call the winds, call the winds.
Let them ride. Snatch the broom
and let it glide away."

Then the winds came, and they came with a roar like an uncontrollable tide, and the land trembled and shook and the old tree rocked, and the winds grew and raged in a great storm and Old Edgar McNezzar could no longer call them back, and even the ancient oak was pulled from the earth and crashed to the ground, and all was darkness.

After the Storm

Edgar was thrown from the highest branch even before the oak came down, while Elzamere beneath, had been caught and buried by the black caging branches of the oak.

The other little folk were safe. The winds had lifted them above the storm clouds, and when the storm abated, the little folk had glided down and landed on the ground. They found Edgar sitting on a clump of wet mud, bruised, battered, and dazed, but still alive.

"It's a wonder we're all safe," he said.

But where was Elzamere? No one knew. They searched the woods in vain.

"You must find shelter in the village amongst the thatched roof cottages," Edgar told the fairies. "I will continue to look for Elzamere and then follow you."

So the little folk set off towards the village. When they arrived, it was late in the day and after the storm, it seemed all the big folk were stopping indoors, and every door was shut. Following a winding, narrow lane they came upon a row of thatched roofed cottages hunched side by side. The fairies flew upwards to inspect the roofs.

"This one is perfect," Dominic decided, "and now we must find some sharp sticks and stones to make a tunnel in the thatch."

They searched about for just the right sticks and stones and started digging.

"We can have a sitting room," said Cora, "with shuttered windows overlooking the cottage gardens and the lane."

"We'll be spoilt," said Poppy, "we even have the heating from the rooms beneath."

Soon the entrance tunnel was complete and they had the beginnings of a room.

"I will use some of the left over straw to make a basket," said Estine. "I've seen Elzamere do it. I bet I can finish it before tomorrow." And she did.

The next day the little folk set out to forage for food amongst the cottage gardens.

"Elzamere would have done this for us," said little Ivy, "weaved baskets, gathered food. I know she was sometimes a bit wicked, but sometimes she was very good to us."

Dominic joined in, "Yes, that's true. I wonder where they are now - Edgar and Elzamere."

In fact, in the clear light of day Edgar was still looking for Elzamere. He had been hunting amongst the churned up soil, the broken trees and twisted roots.

"Are you there Elzamere?" he had called repeatedly. But now he heard a moaning, a coughing, and yet more moaning. The sound was coming from beneath the fallen oak. It was Elzamere moaning.

"It's okay Elzamere I hear you."

He clambered quickly across the branches towards the sounds and began pulling back the twigs one by one. A pale hand appeared, and then an arm and then Elzamere climbed out. Unsteady on her feet she tottered forward. Then with two hands placed against her back, she tried to straighten up.

"Don't talk to me. Never speak to me again," and off she went in her tattered clothes, wobbling back and forth.

"Never speak to me again." Her voice grew softer

as she staggered across the fallen twigs and branches to reach the beech tree. She knocked at the door and soon disappeared within.

Edgar appeared at the opening of the thatch. "I searched for Elzamere," he said, "eventually I found her buried beneath the branches of the oak. She is okay, but she refuses to speak to me. She's staying with her friends, Bead and Silk."

With Edgar's help, the new home took shape. It had several rooms, each with sloping ceilings and windows with straw shutters, just as Cora had wanted. On the outside, the cottage looked much the same, but on the inside, in the thatch, the little folk felt snug and safe. They soon settled into their new way of life - but something was missing.

A Tree

It was Aunt Libby who had spotted that the broomstick was not really a broomstick at all. She turned to Bess and Jodie, "Look I've never seen anything like it," she said, "but it's not a broomstick. It has the little roots like a tree. See it's still got life in it - it's green and springy - look. I bet if you planted it, it would grow. That's what I'd do. I wonder what sort of tree it would be."

Return to the Woods

One evening Edgar said, "Tomorrow we should visit our old home. See if we can find anything of use, and also visit Elzamere. She might speak to you if not to me."

The little folk rose early, took a quick sip of dew, (they needed very little) and set out towards the woods. It was a calm and cloudless day.

They followed beside the cottage walls and passed an old man walking slowly down the path.

"Can he see us?" asked Poppy.

"No, I don't think so," said Edgar.

A child pushed open a squeaky garden gate. A woman smiled a small 'hello' and the child waved back.

"They can't see us, can they?" said Poppy.

"No," said Edgar.

The little folk turned off the lane and entered beneath a gate into a churchyard. Here, the ancient tombstones stood out like giant crooked teeth. A crow was pecking at the moss on one such tooth, and he turned to watch as the little folk made their way through the churchyard.

"The crow can see us," whispered Ivy. "I know him and he's friendly." She waved.

The crow blinked, dipped his head again, shuffled on his feet and went back to picking moss.

The little folk continued through the churchyard, beneath a yew tree that grew in the shadow of the church, up and over a brick wall at the back, then through a line of shrubs and out into the sunshine. They travelled on towards the hills and by early afternoon arrived at their old home ground.

Here was where the oak had stood for centuries. It now lay broken and defeated amongst the wreckage of the storm. The fairies sat down on a fallen branch, while Edgar walked over to the beech tree and knocked at the door. After a moment Elzamere appeared. She looked frail. She took a step outside and looked about.

"How are you?" asked Edgar.

"I will recover." She walked towards the fairies,

"And you - are you all ok?" she asked.

They nodded. Elzamere sat down beside them and for a while, the little folk simply felt each other's sorrow. All was very quiet. It seemed no birds sang today and nothing moved except a few dandelion threads that scattered in the air.

Then the peace was broken. Loud scrunching sounds like the big folk boots crashing through the woods. Suddenly two women loomed above them through the trees. Both had backpacks and one wore a small white hat squashed down upon her head.

"About here I think," said Bess puffing slightly.

Jodie removed her backpack, untied the flap and took out the little broomstick. She placed the broomstick on the ground. Then fumbling through her backpack, she found a small trowel and a bottle of water.

"We found this broomstick in these woods," she said "and this is where we'll plant it."

She knelt down and dug a small hole. The soil, moist and soft, gave easily. Jodie took the broomstick and with its roots facing down she placed it in the ground. Then she heaped the earth back into the hole and covered up the roots.

"There," said Jodie sitting back on her heels.

Bess opened up the bottle and slowly poured

water around the base of the new tree.

After a moment Bess spoke, "Yes, I wonder what sort of tree this will grow to be."

"An oak," said Edgar quietly.

"Well, I think we're done." Jodie took a tissue from her pocket and wiped her hands. The sisters gathered up their things and set off down the hill.

The little people were amazed - a new tree - a new start. One day this oak might grow to replace the old oak. It might even be home for little folk like themselves. They felt the rightness of the moment.

"It seems," said Poppy, "sometimes the big folk are good to us even when they cannot see us."

The fairies turned to Elzamere. "We missed you," they said in turn. Elzamere was touched by their warmth and felt tiny tears welling in her eyes.

"I missed you too."

The Great Adventure

One evening all the little folk were sitting in the main room of their new home in the thatch roof when Edgar began to tell the stories of his youth.

"Falling from the oak was a great shock to us," he said, "but now I remember once before I fell from a tree. It changed my life, and led to a great adventure."

The little folk gathered round to listen.

But there is more to this story than even Edgar knew and what follows is the full story.

At the full moon meeting beneath the sycamore tree, things began much the same as usual. There was talk of upcoming events, trading matters, and one elf spoke of new arrivals, but then the discussion moved along to the subject of the big folk and the little folk felt a stir amongst the goblins and a change of mood.

Knobby the goblin was speaking. "Times are changing. The big folk are getting louder and angrier. I've even seen them screaming and fighting in the streets."

"I've not seen that," an old gnome said brusquely, and he shrugged his bony shoulders.

"You, sir, don't live where I live - they dig up the woods, trample across the land as if they own everything." Then still more harshly, "If you don't know the big folk are selfish, no good, greedy folk ….you've been living on a cloud - and I can tell you, they want rid of us - us the little folk and weren't we here long before them?"

"How do you mean - want rid of us?"

"It's their philo…losphy," he said this word slowly and deliberately. "Their philo…..losphy, - their way of thinking. They think we are not needed and what they don't need they would do away with. They see us as if we were termites."

"What's that?" asked a small fairy sitting on a root.

"Ants boy, ants.

Another fairy spoke up, "Surely that's not true. They mostly don't even see us, and in any case I like the big folk. Some of them are kind."

"You think that because you're a fairy. I'm sorry but I can't take the word of a fairy against my own experience. You fairies have no idea."

The fairy looked offended. "I'm not being funny," she continued, "but - 'angry and noisy' aren't they words used to describe goblins."

"Fight fire with fire."

The atmosphere was tense, electric, as if a storm might brew.

Then Gromley, an elderly gnome from the Uplands spoke, "We must not interfere with big folk, it is not our way. They must learn their own lessons. Only the elements can help them understand."

"The Elements? What do you mean by the elements?" asked an imp impatiently.

"The wind, rain, fire - the weather basically. I think perhaps, we might consider continuing this discussion at the next full moon. I call this meeting to a close."

The groups of little folk started to break up, but the goblins stood their ground.

"No more meetings beneath the sycamore tree," Knobby muttered. "No more discussions. Time for action."

The young Edgar and his brothers lived comfortable enough - fishing and foraging, mostly in the woods, but sometimes in the gardens of the big folk. To be fair they worked hard in the gardens - amongst the sprouting vegetables, pulling out weeds, which they found quite tasty. When the seasons came to ripen the plants the gnomes would take their share of carrots, beans, peas and berries. There was enough and more to fill their bellies.

Sometimes the brothers stole nuts from the bird feeders, much to the annoyance of the birds and the squirrels. These nuts would make a tasty pudding, usually made with water, but sometimes with the milk from the cat's saucer. One gnome would do something to distract the cat, like blowing a raspberry, and another gnome would nip in quick and tip the milk from the saucer into their pudding pot. No cat could catch a gnome, and the cat would merely be seen as a silly thing chasing its own tail.

In those days summers were good, but the winters were very cold. The brothers would collect twigs to make little fires, bed down in abandoned birds' nests and sometimes gather on the rooftops to warm themselves against the smoking chimney pots.

Edgar was the youngest of the brothers and when Ma and Pa had been alive, he had been the favourite. Ma and Pa had simply disappeared one day. This is something that just happens with old gnomes. It is sad, and no one really knows where they go. But it has been known for them to reappear when least expected.

For the most part the brothers got on very well together, but being a little jealous of Edgar the youngest and the favourite, they were not always kind to him, and it seemed to them he was just a little too clever and a little too odd. Gnomes are known to be odd, but Edgar would often appear to be listening to the winds as though they had something special to say to him and him alone. Of course, his brothers knew that the winds could speak, but they thought - "well who listens nowadays?" So they would call Edgar "Windy Edgar" and blow raspberries in his face and laugh until the poor lad wandered off alone.

In truth, Edgar was not easily upset and he enjoyed his own company. He would sit high in a tree and listen to the winds. However, there are winds and there are winds: the summer softy winds, the harsh hill winds of winter, the west winds, the southern winds, the eastern winds and the chill north wailing winds, and each would speak to him in turn. However, on this day the winds were snapping at one another.

"My turn, my turn, - move round - move round - beat it. I've had enough. I was here first."

Edgar thought this argument very funny and began to laugh out loud. This was not a good thing to do - you should take the elements very seriously. Thwack went a shrill, indignant wind. Edgar went spinning off the branch, fell to the ground, banged his head on a hard, outstretched root and lay very still in the shadow of the tree.

"Wake him up. Wake him up," a kind wind blew gently on his face, but he did not wake. Sometime later, a mouse came scratching round. It snuffled round his ears and breathed into his nostrils. Edgar, suddenly roused, sat up and the mouse, a timid thing, scurried off into the undergrowth.

"Where am I?" said Edgar in a daze. "Who am I?" He held his aching head. Red and green lights flashed and zigzagged about him. He felt sick.

"I remember nothing."

He stood up, looked down at his boots, and studied them as if looking for a clue.

"I will follow this path." He stumbled forward like a drunken gnome. The path led downwards and grew narrow. Up above the trees entwined their branches and all but blotted out the light. Edgar moved on, trampling over pebbles, twigs, thorns and the knotty threads of grass and leaves. Poor Edgar, caught by jagged things, ensnared by brambles, tripped and fell face down into a mass of crawling giant ants. But Edgar fought back - kicking, punching and then, scrambling to his feet he staggered forward once again.

Edgar traipsed through woods, high and low for what seemed hours. He grew weary. He had lost his memory, lost his way and now was going nowhere. But then a hopeful sign, "I smell water," he thought. Suddenly Edgar saw a clearing leading to a stretch of water. He rushed forward, dropped down, cupped his hands and drank.

"Who am I...?" he asked, and looking down he

saw the image of a face. One raindrop fell and broke across the dark reflection, and then another and another. Raindrops dribbled on his neck. He looked up to see black clouds and lightning flashes. Now the rain was falling fast. Edgar moved towards the trees and with his hat pulled down and his arms tight across his buttoned coat, he waited. Thunder boomed. Crash, bang. Edgar took a quick sideways step and slipped, and falling on his back across the slippery grass, he rolled into the water. For several moments he disappeared beneath the swell and when he reappeared, he was further out, struggling and kicking. A small branch floated by. Edgar grabbed at it and hung on blindly as it rolled and dipped. But suddenly the branch tipped up and slid beneath the waves. Down, down, swoosh, down, down, then through a cold, dark water tunnel, and all at once, the branch popped up above the water level. Edgar, still clinging on, gasped for breath, coughed and spluttered.

He found himself floating in small, dark pool. Beyond the pool, blurry lights showed the vague outlines of a cave. He heard dripping sounds and shuffling echoes and all about was cold and gloom. Looking upwards he saw blackness with just a few points of light like distant stars. Edgar paddled to one side and dragged himself up and over onto the cave floor. He was dazed and shocked. But now there was a smell. It was something rancid, something rotten and the caves reeked of it. Edgar shivered.

"Where am I?" he asked hopelessly. As he slowly stood he saw his own shadow cast before him. Edgar turned around. A tall goblin (one of the taller breed) with a flaming torch, was staring down at him. The goblin's eyes were red veined and set in wrinkled sockets. Its flaccid lips were quivering.

"Who are you?"

"I don't remember," Edgar managed a reply.

"I see. That means you're a worker. Come on man - back to camp with you."

Just then a large grey rat appeared. It had been there all along.

"Come boy," said the goblin to the rat. The rat bared its yellow teeth.

Everything was disgusting to Edgar: the smells, the bat droppings encrusted on the ground and this rat, scratching, sniffing and dribbling from both ends.

Edgar shivered.

"Follow me," the goblin said and now Edgar felt the rat's hot, hell-stinking breath upon his back.

Some way on the goblin turned around. "Down boy - good boy," he told the rat. "Go boy," and the rat rasped, dribbled and scurried off.

"There, take your place." The goblin moved his head to indicate a cave opening where a faint light flickered.

Edgar, wet and shivering, grimly shuffled on. He came upon a group of sorry souls hunched around a fire. With eyes closed, they were blindly slurping food from bowls.

"There's no more. No more," they said. Then they threw their crude clay bowls amongst empty mugs that lay about the floor, and one by one looked up at Edgar.

"Who are you?"

"I know not," he said.

"Ah then you are one of us. Come sit with us. There is nothing else."

He moved forward to the fire, sat down, and then in weariness he slept.

Next day the five worker gnomes were six. They walked through a long dark corridor of stone to their place of work. Each took a pickaxe and set to work. Just two goblins were there to oversee this crew. These gnomes were strong in body, but they were weak in mind. One goblin stood back watching, picking his teeth, whilst his ratty pet sniffed the air and shuffled round his feet. The other goblin strutted up and down. He leaned against the wall, craned his neck, checked his watch from time to time and wrote down figures in a notebook.

The gnomes struck their pick axes hard against the cave wall to shatter stone from stone. Then they hefted the broken bits onto a mighty barrow.

This day, the goblin with the rat, was in a cold and angry mood, in truth, he was always in a cold and angry mood.

"Oy you lazy, lowlife, worthless lot. Put your backs into it." He pointed at a gnome struggling to push the barrow.

"What did I say?" and he kicked the poor lad who slipped and overturned the barrow.

"You fool," said the goblin. The young gnome

hunched down, quickly set the wheelbarrow right and filled it up again.

The other goblin spoke. "We can't afford delays. It's the schedule you know, the schedule. Swot, I can manage here you go check the ventilation holes. Then you can prepare the gruel and pies. I'll see you later to inspect the vats."

The goblin knew the routine. He didn't need Stark to tell him. He turned, spat, shrugged his shoulders and set off down corridor to the pool cave where Edgar had first arrived. His foul smelling rat followed on behind.

He found his stick for poking things, stuck it in his teeth and clambered up the cave walls. Goblins are agile with broad, sucker-like hands, good for gripping stone. Swot knew the well-worn foot holes, but still it took quite some time to climb the rock face to the top. He scrambled sideways along the runnels of the roof, where bats, hanging upside down, were wheezing in their sleep. The vents were blocked and darkly caked with droppings. Swot jabbed his stick to clear the holes and bits and lumps fell passed him to the ground. Fresh air and light filtered in. The goblin wrinkled up his nose, shifted round and slowly clambered down.

His next duty was to prepare the workers' breakfast. Their food consisted of a gruel made from fungus and straw and little pies made from herbs and weeds and sometimes potato peelings and a brew to drink made from fermented roots. The brew was the most important thing. It was a brew to stop the workers thinking, to make them docile and to forget.

The gnomes now returned to their cave for breakfast. Swot brought in a pot of gruel, and a small pile of pies.

"Here's your gruel, your pies. Come on you

worthless lot," and they each held out their clay bowls. Later that day they would receive their brew.

Elsewhere in the caves, things were going on. Knobby the goblin was speaking with his brothers, Stark and Grimweed.

"I need a progress report. When will the new storage space be ready?"

"August the 15th," said Stark briefly.

"And the brew does it work?"

"It's been tested successfully on the workers. They work hard, but remember nothing of themselves."

"And the vat - will there be sufficient brew?"

"We need more volunteers to gather roots. We do have a stockpile of roots, but we need more."

"Unfortunately, as you know, most fairy folk say they won't interfere in anything to do with the big folk. They do not sympathize with our cause. Some still believe that big folk are decent." Knobby laughed loudly; his cheeks and small upturned nose turned pink. "Those meeting under the sycamore tree - what a waste of time." He continued, "I have a meeting this afternoon with Lord and Lady Flanelle. I believe they are sympathetic to our cause, after all, this is their home and we are their good tenants. Perhaps they will provide funds to buy a few more goblin 'volunteers' to gather roots."

"What about abducting some more gnome workers?" Grimweed suggested keenly.

"No. There are too many questions asked and those worker gnomes must never be seen above ground."

The group of six barely looked at one another as they finished their meal.

"Where am I?" asked Edgar.

"Who knows," said a shadowy figure to his left, "we remember nothing."

But after a while, Edgar raised his head. "I do remember something," he said gazing upwards - "I remember light, daylight."

The other gnomes stared at him. After just a little while, one poor soul spoke up.

"I too remember something, but just one thing - I loved someone - my wife, but where and when?"

The group listened to this sad young man and in the darkness of the cave felt his sadness too, and in the darkness of their minds faint images emerged - memories.

Another spoke, "I remember one thing too - being strong - strong in body, but also strong in mind."

One by one - "I remember singing and friendship."

"I remember freedom."

"I remember good food."

Edgar stood. "Yes I remember now - my name is Edgar McNezzar and I have brothers and a home."

"I am Brook," said another with tears welling in his eyes. "And Rosy is my wife."

Then a lad spoke out, "Yes, I remember - I am Robin and I am a carpenter."

"And I am Duncan, a baker."

"I'm Jasper a musician and a song smith."

"And I am Guffrey, a fisherman."

Lord and Lady Flanelle lived high up in the caves. Their chambers were an elaborate affair. In the main room an enormous crystal chandelier set with candles, hung down from a stalactite in the centre of the ceiling. Its light cast rainbows on a pool beneath and glistened on the beads and threads of moisture that trickled down the limestone walls. Huge wall pots with red and yellow fungus blooms, like exotic flowers, were set in staggered lines from floor to ceiling. The furniture was grand with green and copper coloured sofas, plump moss cushions, and polished stools and tables carved from stalagmites.

Lady Flanelle entered the room, - swept in - made her entrance. She wore a gown of white stitched with tiny silken flowers. Her hair was piled high upon her head, and she wore gold eye shadow.

"Gold," she would say with a flutter of her lashes, "to match my eyes and hair."

Lord Flanelle entered. He was stout and short - shorter than his wife, but he stood tall in that he knew himself to be a goblin of power and influence. He wore a purple knitted waistcoat and nicely tailored trousers.

Knobby entered. The goblin looked very dowdy by comparison.

"Please take a seat," said the lady graciously. "No not there," she pointed. "That stool." Then she settled herself down upon a sofa and the lord stood tall.

A large caterpillar crept into the room and cat-like slipped onto the lady's lap.

"Ah Pricilla, my dear Siamese caterpillar." She stroked her pet, turned, and then, picked up a small brass bell and rang it.

A goblin entered. He was a short, portly, red-faced goblin.

"You rang madam."

"Yes Giles. Pricilla is hungry. Please bring some leaves." Giles left the room.

The lord turned to Knobby, but could not remember his name.

"Well how are things? How can we help you?"

"I think you will sympathise with our cause," said Knobby straight away. "I understand you are not so keen on the big folk hereabouts."

The lord sniffed and shifted on his feet. "No no, I'm fine with the big folk."

Knobby looked surprised. This meeting might not go as he had hoped.

"It's true they are tall - the big folk - and tallness can be offensive, but on the whole we get on well with them."

Knobby pressed on, "I must inform you that we - the First Order of the Goblins - consider them to be destructive and harmful to all little folk."

"Yes well … I've heard that said. You think them harmful, but really we are quite safe here, even if a bomb should drop, and even your chambers down below, are safe."

The two men looked at one another.

"I wish this fellow would disappear," thought the lord, yawning and tapping at his watch.

"What a little prig," thought Knobby, but he smiled.

The lord continued. "Yes we have had much dealing with the big folk. In the past, we made our fortune through dealings with them. You would be surprised how like us many of them are."

"Greedy like you," thought Knobby.

"As you probably know parts of these lands still have small amounts of gold. But we knew something else. We knew where it was, and for a price, we were prepared to go into business with the big folk. We informed them of where they could unearth some nuggets and in what rivers they could pan for gold. They did all the work and paid us handsomely in gold dust."

"And you were quite prepared to reveal yourselves to the big folk?"

"It was easy. After all - like attracts like. Yes we have friends in high places."

"And," said Lady Flanelle "that's how we can afford to live in these beautiful caves," she gestured and gazed smugly round the room, "and we still have so much gold dust left."

The servant returned with an enormous leaf and gave it to the lady.

"Here darling." Her pet rolled over and started munching on the leaf.

After a moment, Knobby spoke again. "Lord and Lady Flanelle I can see you have much experience in the world of business. Would you be prepared to let us have a small loan so that we can carry out our plans to make the big folk a little less angry, less destructive, but most of all - less tall?"

The lord hesitated, "A loan? How much do you want?"

"Twenty thousand speckles of gold dust," said Knobby coolly.

"That's no small loan," replied the lord. He turned and walked a few paces towards the pool. He turned again to face Knobby.

"Yes, I believe we can lend you twenty thousand speckles. After one year you will have to pay us back three times that amount - in other words, sixty thousand speckles of gold dust."

"Sixty thousand speckles?" Knobby was shocked, but after a moment, he continued. "Yes perhaps we can do business on your terms."

He thanked the lord and lady and left.

The group of six gnomes agreed that the goblins must not know that they had regained their memories. They huddled together whispering, exchanging thoughts and spoke of feelings once lost, now reclaimed.

"I remember," said Robin, "one evening I was walking home when I was set upon by goblins. They held me down and made me drink the very brew we have here. It was bitter and I tried to spit it out, but they kept pouring it down my throat. Everything became dark and I felt dead inside. Now we drink the stuff all the time. It's all we have to quench our thirst and it no longer tastes so bitter."

"I too must have been abducted," said Guffrey, "I had a good day's fishing, and then went for a drink - one or two in fact. I remember leaving the tavern and then nothing - I remember nothing."

Jasper the musician spoke, "Yes, I was on the road when set upon by goblins."

"And I was baking bread, working through the night to have it ready for the morning. They sneaked into the bakery, knocked me to the ground and forced me to drink the stuff."

Each one of them had much the same story apart from Edgar. In turn they were moved by grief, anger, rage, and then by hope.

"We are six strong gnomes - we can beat the goblins, and I shall see my Rosy once again."

"And how many goblins are there? I've only seen two?" said Edgar.

"It varies. They come and go. They work in shifts. There's one goblin, I think his name is Knobby - he seems to be in charge."

"Shush, the goblin's back," Robin warned.

"Line up boys - follow me," said Swot sourly and, in what seemed like a very docile fashion, they followed back to work.

When Knobby returned to his chamber, he was

still thinking about the meeting with Lord and Lady Flanelle.

"Those greedy creeps. If they think they can make me look a fool they are mistaken and what did they mean 'they have friends in high places'? Could I trust them? Or will they turn to their big folks 'friends' for help if I don't repay the loan?"

He certainly needed the gold to pay his goblin workers, but he had no intention of repaying such a vast amount of money.

"It will be so simple to add the brew to the water supply. After all, the waters of the reservoir flow through these caves. Docile - dumb-downed big folk, that's what we need."

Knobby called his assistant to his room.

"Walter."

"Yes Sir."

"The contract we prepared - it looks very good. I know they will sign it and hand over the gold dust."

"Yes sir."

"Ask my brothers Stark and Grimweed to join us. We have business to do."

Later that afternoon the contract was signed by Knobby and then by the Lord and Lady Flanelle and the loan of twenty thousand speckles was weighed and handed over to the goblins.

When the gnomes returned for their evening meal, they set about making plans for escape.

"We should find out how the land lies." Edgar told the group how he had arrived through the water channel "and if we can make it back there - there's fresh water to drink."

"It's always dark and they won't be expecting us to be moving round at night. The goblins sleep - you can hear them snoring in the dark, but the rat…" said Guffrey.

"Perhaps it will it take the brew from our mugs?" suggested Brook.

They decided to soak the pies from their evening meal in the brew and feed this to the rat.

Much later in the night, they could hear the goblins snoring. They stuffed the soaked pies in their mugs and put them in their pockets, and then with great stealth, the six gnomes crept through the cave to its opening.

Outside a dim light flickered from one of the many torches that were fixed against the walls. The goblins relit the flames throughout the day. This provided a light but, also to goblins, it was a way of telling the time as the flames would falter only after so many hours. The gnomes moved on. Soon they were close enough to see the rat. It was sleeping, curled up, its eyes shut tight. It twitched and Guffrey at the front held up an arm to signal, "Stop". They froze. The rat turned over as if, in so deep a sleep, he really did not want to know. Beyond the rat a guard was stretched out and snoring loudly. Beside him lay his spear. Guffrey waved them on and as he passed the guard, he picked up the spear.

Then Edgar took the lead and they all followed down the corridor to the pool where he had first landed in this hellhole. They took out their mugs, emptied them of pies, rinsed them, and then they drank the clear, fresh water from the pool. For all, but Edgar, it was their first taste of pure water for many months.

After a moment Jasper said, "I remember, I've

been here before."

"Yes," said Guffrey, "I have a hazy memory. A great catfish swam up this channel. It wore a harness - yes and it was hauling barrels through the water. I remember we had to drag the barrels ashore with nets and ropes then roll them to a storage space. - do you remember?" He looked around.

"We do," said Duncan.

"The ropes and nets - where would they be?" asked Edgar.

"In the same storage area, which is somewhere along from where we now work. There's a turning to the right," said Guffrey.

"With ropes and nets and may be a pickaxe or two we might climb our way up towards the lights above and if need be - dig ourselves out," said Brook.

Duncan looked around. "Shush - someone's coming."

A smell of rat soured the air and from somewhere close, came scratching, rasping sounds. The rat loomed into view. It stood jittery; its nose twitched and its beady eyes darted back and forth. Robin grabbed his pie from the ground and lobbed it at the rat. It zinged above its whiskers and fell from sight. A glint of yellowed fangs, claws broken, grooved - extended, and the rat reared up. It tottered and was set to pounce. Guffrey swiftly raised his spear, and in one deadly movement, thrust forwards and up. The spear pierced the creature's heart. Its eyes bulged. It squealed a tortured squeal, writhed, fell and thud - the rat was dead.

But now two goblins, waving spears, were fast approaching. Guffrey withdrew the bloodied spear from the dead rat and as the first goblin lunged, Guffrey shifted on his feet and parried. Then Jasper ducking sideways tripped the goblin and snatched the fallen spear. The second goblin followed just behind. He shrieked across his shoulder to where other goblins were emerging from the gloom.

Guffrey, Duncan, Edgar, Brook, Jasper and Robin were six desperate gnomes and fighting with their fists, knees, elbows and spears the goblins were defeated. Just one goblin disappeared into darkness. The others lay winded, dazed or unconscious on the ground.

The six gnomes took the spears, ran back along

the passageway and entered the work cave. Here Brook found a pickaxe beneath the wheelbarrow and picked it up. Then moving on they took a turning to the right.

"Yes this is where we brought the barrels in. I recognize the smell for one thing." Indeed the air was thick and foul. "Over there," Guffrey pointed, "behind the barrels - are ropes and nets."

They found a rope, a net and with the pickaxe they were set to go, yet as they turned to leave, their eyes were drawn towards a door at the far end, and suddenly they knew, that from behind this door, through gaps above, gaps below and cracks within, a stink was seeping out.

"Let's get out," said Guffrey.

Returning to the pool, they saw the rat, now rigid on its back with a frozen sneer and a mush of blood encrusted on its fur. The defeated goblins were nowhere to be seen.

"Now we must be like mountaineers," said Guffrey looking up.

Duncan hesitated, "Yes, but I think I suffer from vertigo – I just don't like heights. "

Robin looked at him, "Oh no, that's bad….."

"What do you mean," growled Guffrey.

"Well I've never tried climbing up so high."

"What's the matter with you? Do you want to be clubbed to death or eaten by a rat?"

The baker looked about. "Okay let's go."

Still carrying the equipment and a flaming torch they climbed one-handed up the cave walls. Brook stopped to chip a foot hole in the stone. The clinking sounds echoed through the caves. But now there were other sounds - jabbering and scratching sounds. The gnomes glanced down and saw just below the ghostly grey-green faces of the goblins. Guffrey, the fisherman, took aim and cast the net. It spread loosely and dropped away. A goblin shrieked, trapped and netted and struggling within the net with his flaming torch, he fell, and like the boulders of an avalanche one goblin fell upon another and then another. It seemed all the goblins were falling to the ground. There were cries of fear, and in a moment, a thud, an echo, and then silence, complete silence.

The six gnomes turned and quickly set off again. But now before them they saw a flat rock face that appeared to rise straight up.

"Impossible to climb," said Duncan craning his neck to look up.

"I'll handle this," said Guffrey. He knotted one end of the rope to make a loop and threw it overhead towards a jutting rock - a ledge above. Once, it missed. He threw it up again, and this time the rope slipped over, caught and held tight. He placed his spear sideways through his belt and gripping firmly to the rope he climbed up, pushing with his feet hard against the cave wall until he was able to swing himself up and over to the ledge. For a moment, he lay belly down on the slimy ridge. He cast his eyes down to where the others watched and beyond them to the depths where flames flickered weakly at the bottom of the cave. Now, up above the bats were stirring and Guffrey heard a low squeaking sound. The squeaks turned to screeches and then a whizzing sound and suddenly the bats, with gaping mouths and hungry fangs seemed to drop from nothing into sight and back again to nothing. They were not small creatures as they would be to you or me. To a gnome they were large and fearsome. Guffrey drew his spear, rose, and with the skill of one who had done this kind of thing before, he jabbed and yelled. Then Edgar, with his flaming torch gripped between his teeth, clambered up the rope. The others followed. Soon all the gnomes were standing on the ledge fighting off the bats. It was enough. The bats dropped out of sight into nothingness.

For several seconds no one spoke, and the only sound, above their own laboured breath, was the dripping echoes of the caves. Gradually they turned about. How far had they come? How far must they climb? The six gnomes strained their eyes to see. It seemed the ledge they were standing on followed round and led towards an opening in the cave wall.

Edgar stepped forward. Yes, his torch revealed the beginning of a corridor. "Let see where it takes us."

They marched in two by two. The single torch light cast its eerie shadows against the rough stone walls and small gusts of air whistled through the corridor.

Some way along Edgar pointed. "Look, there's a door on the right."

Jasper tried the handle in vain. "It's locked."

Suddenly from somewhere further down they heard screams and cries for help. A lady, a damsel in distress, was screaming.

Without hesitation, the gnomes ran forward. At the passage end they saw something that was very odd. A large caterpillar was scratching at a door, and now it was clear that the screams were coming from within. Edgar rushed forward, tried the handle and pushed open the door.

On the other side a picture of horror awaited them. In the centre of the room a goblin lay face down in a pool. The water spooled pink with blood. To one side a lady was kneeling on the floor. She clutched her side as blood trickled down the creases of her gown. Robin reached out to her. He held her in his arms. Brook rushed forward and pulled the goblin from the water, but clearly, it was too late. He was dead.

"I too am dead," the lady murmured.

"No, no," cried Robin, "we will help."

He thought she could have been his mother and he felt tears welling in his eyes.

"Look after Pricilla … Where is Giles? …Go - use the fire escape. Save yourselves." Then she died.

For some moments, they simply stared at the scene of horror. Then Guffrey said, "Let's get out of here."

"Who's Pricilla? Who is Giles? What fire escape?"

So now, they hunted round looking for a Pricilla, for a Giles and for a fire escape.

The kitchen contained a large water pot, several cooking pots full of weeds, an oven in the wall, and an empty larder. In another room, they found a round bed and wardrobes full of clothes, but no Pricilla, no Giles and no fire escape. Yet another room was empty altogether, save for tiny specks of golden dust on the floor and a few empty sacks. The gnomes were mystified.

When they returned to the main room, no one noticed the caterpillar hanging by a thread of silk from the chandelier above.

"If there's a fire escape we can be out of here soon." Brook turned and looked about.

Edgar was staring at the wall pots. He noticed

that the fungus blooms were squashed and broken and dusted with tiny specks of gold.

"Yes, I get it," Edgar said at last. "The fire escape - we can climb up these fungus pots, up and out. It looks like they've been used recently."

He was right. "Come on," he told the others. He climbed up the pots and at the top he found an opening - a skylight. It was darkly smeared with grass and mould. One by one the gnomes climbed up and out to freedom.

Now, in the daylight they had to cover their eyes and blink and the strangeness of the soft grass beneath their feet and the clear fresh air was almost overwhelming. Gradually adjusting to the brightness, they found they were standing on high ground and it was morning - early dawn.

"We are free." Jasper raised his arms, stretched and turned as if to greet the world.

"We are not dreaming - this is real." Brook was near to tears.

"Yes," said Duncan as he held his head with both hands. He was feeling dizzy.

They looked at one another properly for the first

time, at their long hair, tangled beards, yellow hooded eyes, and the grimy layered creases on their faces. All were gaunt and their clothes hung loose, worn, torn and dirty.

"Well we are a fine looking bunch," declared Duncan.

Yet somehow, beneath each sorry sight, they could see the true gnome. Jasper was a lanky lad; Brook, blue eyed and most likely handsome beneath the dirt; Robin eager, sensitive; Guffrey, strong and honest; Duncan good humoured, and Edgar, well he was just the young Edgar. They rubbed their faces, knowing that each was as grimy as the next. Then they took a breath. To the east, the sun rose and cast a brilliant light upon the reservoir beneath. To the west, they saw a shallow valley, trees, hills, and houses in the distance. Then what was this? Quite far away, a small fat figure, carrying a sack, was making slow progress puffing up a hill. He disappeared from sight into the shadow of a tree, reappeared, and then disappeared again.

"Stop!" cried Robin.

"Thief! Murderer!" cried the baker.

"We'll catch him. He will have to pay for it. We'll take him to the authorities and tell them of the other crimes too - how we were abducted and drugged. They'll shut that place down, put those goblins into prison and throw the keys away. Yes we'll get justice."

The six gnomes ran down the hillside across the valley and up towards the goblin. They followed through the trees, through a clearing, and finally they caught up with the puffing little fellow and grabbed him by the shoulders. His sack flew one way and he another, and crowding round, they pinned him to the ground.

"Murderer! Thief!"

The goblin was winded and struggling for breath. He coughed, and spluttered and it was clear he was going nowhere.

"We have a length of rope. We can tie you up."

"No, no," he coughed and blubbered. "Please don't take me back to Knobby."

What was he talking about? They pulled the fellow up. Duncan grabbed him by the shoulders. "Do you deny that you are a murderer and thief? And in this sack here - the proof. I'll wager you killed to steal this sack of gold dust."

"No." The goblin was shaking. His puffy face was red and sweaty.

Edgar glared. "Then we shall see." He opened up the sack and looked inside. He looked again.

"Let us see the evidence," said Robin grimly.

Edgar tipped up the sack. There was no gold dust - but a flask of water, a large quantity of crusty rolls, tomatoes, carrots and a very long sausage fell across the ground.

"Oh!" After a moment, "So you killed for food and food alone. - We know, we have just come from the caves, where you so brutally killed two goblins - a gentleman - we found him face down in a pool - and the lady too, she ….." Edgar could not finish.

The goblin looked horrified. "The Lord and Lady Flanelle…!" and he set to wailing. "They have killed my Lady and my Lord."

"Who have?"

Giles tried to pull himself together.

"Knobby and his evil men."

After a moment, he began again. "Lord Flanelle," he sniffed and rubbed his wet face, "…..made a great deal of money through doing business with some mining people - in fact they were big folk."

The gnomes gasped, but they let Giles continue.

"The Lord and Lady Flanelle had stacks of gold dust, sacks of it locked in a storeroom within the apartment, and yesterday Knobby came to see the Lord to borrow money. He said he had a plan to bring the big folk down to size, so he said, and asked for a loan of twenty thousand speckles of gold dust.

Later in the day, Knobby returned, accompanied by three goblins, and one goblin produced an impressive looking contract for the loan, with a lot of small print, I must say. But all seemed in order. It was signed on the dotted line."

The baker spoke. "Excuse me for interrupting, but do you mind if we have some water, a roll and perhaps some sausage?"

"Of course, help yourselves."

"And what was this plot against the big folk?" asked Edgar.

"I believe, but I could be wrong, their plan had something to do with the reservoir. I heard rumours from other goblins in the cave that they wanted to add something to the reservoir so that when the big folk drank the water they would be milder, more gentle people, more like us little folk."

Now everything fell into place.

"That's the brew. It does more than make you gentle - it makes you dead from the neck up. It is poison. It was tested on us - it's evil stuff." They told the goblin briefly, what had happened to them.

"If it wasn't for Edgar here, we would still be down there. But what happened to you next? What were you doing running away with this food?"

The goblin continued. "Knobby and his two brothers brought their own scales to measure out twenty thousand speckles. His brother, Grimweed, as sour a looking a goblin as I've ever seen, set the scales down on the floor, and I brought in the sacks of gold dust from the storeroom, but however many sacks I brought and set upon the scales it only registered just under twenty thousand speckles. At last, they took the sacks and left. However, they forgot to take the scales - so I stood on them to test them, and once again, they registered just under twenty thousand speckles. Well I know I weigh more than that, and then I realized that Knobby and his brothers were dishonest. My Lord and Lady would hear none of it - so convinced they were that they would get a good return for their money. I decided to seek advice. I took an empty sack from the storeroom. Yes, there was a little gold dust on it, and I filled it up with food for the journey. I knew this was no hardship for the Lord and Lady - they were due to receive a delivery of food today." Once again, he looked crestfallen and sobbed, but then continued. "They had always stated that they have friends in high places - meaning the big folk - and I remembered they once mentioned the miners lived in a large blue house up there to the west. I knew it was a risk to seek them out, but I knew no other way to help. I brought a copy of the contract - see…." he said. "But now it serves no purpose. I guess Knobby and his evil men must have returned to commit the crime soon after I had climbed out by the fire escape and then they must have left again just before you got there." His eyes rolled and he clasped his hands.

"They'll be after me, that you can be sure of, and you too. They'll be after you."

Robin spoke kindly to the goblin. "You are one of us now, and we must stick together."

Giles looked relieved, but then he wondered if

they should still seek out the big folk miners - the 'friends in high places'.

"They might sympathize and take our side against the murderous goblins," said Giles.

But Edgar decided, "I don't think we should waste our time on half a chance."

Giles held back from speaking. He was still convinced his Lordship's worthy friends would assist in seeking out revenge.

"We should be moving on. When we reach a village we can seek help from other gnomes," Edgar reasoned. "Let's put the spears in the sack with the remaining food and flask. We can carry the pickaxe and the rope separately"

They set off towards the woods, then crossed the hills and followed down towards a valley, where a stream flowed beside an orchard. Jasper filled the water flask, and gazed back towards the others. "We must smell like rotten vegetables."

The gnomes jumped in the water. They immersed themselves and splashed about, and in the fresh, clear water, the fresh air and bright sunshine, suddenly they knew they were alive.

"I could do with a bucket full of suds and a scrubbing brush," said Duncan. He rubbed his matted hair.

"Cold water and a nettle leaf, is just fine for now," said Robin splashing water on his face.

"Never had a bath with all my clothes on before," said Brook.

The six gnomes, in dripping clothes, crossed over to the other side and climbed out. Giles dragged himself slowly through the water with his shoes and socks above his head, and then clambered up the bank. He shook his trousered legs and replaced his socks and shoes.

There was no time to waste. They travelled on through the shadows of the trees fearing goblins from the caves might be tracking them.

In fact, for the moment, they had less to fear than they believed. Knobby had lost all his goblins apart from his two brothers Grimweed and Stark and his assistant, Walter. He did not know in what direction Giles might flee, and he knew nothing of the fire escape.

Back at the caves, Knobby addressed Walter and his two brothers.

"Go search the villages. Act as spies - ask if strangers have been seen. We must find the gnomes and that butler Giles. Go now and return with news. I will stay here to make plans."

Unfortunately for Knobby: - the gnomes and Giles set off towards the West; Stark to the South; Grimweed to the East and Walter to the North.

The goblin and the six escapee gnomes were making good progress. They travelled through the trees, beneath the hedges, and then along the ditches. In the evening, they entered a thickly wooded region, and walked on until dusk set in. Then they stopped and camped. After finishing the food, too tired talk, they sat in silence.

"What's that noise?" Jasper pointed, "Over there…."

A moving shape - a shadowed figure - a lean, mean fox was stalking through the trees towards them. The gnomes, no strangers to foxes, began jumping up and down. They made loud growling noises like angry dogs and Guffrey waved a spear. "I know how to use this."

Yet the fox, too late for food, was bored. He had no taste for gnomes. He sniffed, turned tail, lifted up his leg to mark his territory and loped away.

The gnomes slept a deep, exhausted and dreamless sleep.

Next day they walked on stopping only now and then to pick fruits and nuts. Early afternoon they left the woods and ventured out into a bright sunlit field where sheep were standing in the shade of a single tree.

The travellers tramped through the field over to the other side. Here a lane led, one way, up towards the hills, the other way down towards the valleys. A horse and cart was just now drawing up the hill with what looked like an overload of hay.

With the rattle of the cart and the clip clop of the horse's hooves close upon them, Guffrey spoke out, "Listen. If we quickly climb that overhanging tree branch we can jump off and catch a lift as the hay cart goes by."

They were up the tree in a flash and Guffrey called: "one, two, three, and jump."

Not quite together, they jumped and fell into the hay.

"Better than walking," said Edgar sitting down and stretching out his legs.

"Any water left?" Duncan asked, "I'm parched."

There was just enough for a single swig each and they passed the flask around, and then in the easy rhythm of the cart, the gnomes sat back and dozed.

"Don't snore," Duncan nudged Guffrey, "you'll spook the horse."

Guffrey was now wide-awake. "Better look for road signs."

After several miles, a road sign stated 'To the village of Bucklesweet' and showed a fork to the left. The cart stopped to take the right hand fork.

"Let's hop it," Brook pointed to the sign, "I know this Uplands village just ahead," and the gnomes were off.

The village of Bucklesweet was a busy place full of big folk, but the gnomes were unconcerned about big folk.

Brook looked round, "Yes, I've been here before. I think Gromley and another elderly gnome live hereabouts. Let's see if we can find a gnome who can direct us."

They were now walking along a terraced road with small, front gardens. No. 1 Cotta Lane had dahlias; No. 2, had marigolds; No. 3, had lilac; No. 4, had buddleia, lavender, old-fashioned rambling roses, poppies, geraniums, ivy, stinging nettles and brambles.

"We're in luck," said Brook confidently, "gnomes must be living here." Just as he said this, an old gnome emerged from behind the buddleia bush.

"Excuse me," said Brook.

"Arternoon," the old gent was leaning on his cane, "Just looking for worms and grubs, and you - you be looking for a mountain, with that rope and pickaxe…... None round here I know of," he added with a toothless grin.

"You'd be surprised," Duncan quipped.

"And what can I do for you?" he moved his head, as if he could hear more clearly from one side.

Brook asked, "Do you know if an elderly gnome called Gromley lives around here?"

"I'm a little deaf. Gromley you say." He took his time. He scratched his cap, rubbed his beard, and studied his walking stick awhile.

"Six young men in such a hurry," he said at last. Then he pointed with his stick and waved it. "Up yonder, in a shed, or barn, back of farm. That's Gromley's place."

"Thank you very much."

"You're welcome."

As they turned away Edgar said, "Poor old gnome, he couldn't count. We are seven - oh no - where's Giles, the goblin, he's gone."

They walked some way along the lane. Gradually they became aware of the smell of dung and the clattering of hooves. Around the next bend, they saw a lad strolling along behind a line of cows. The cows just now turned off towards the entrance of a farm. The gnomes followed quickly through as the gate was closing.

The giant beasts squelched across mounds of mud and dung, then clattered over cobblestones towards a milking shed and disappeared within.

"They are gone. Mucky here isn't it." Duncan looked down at his already scruffy, muddy boots, as if they were his best.

"Let's look around," said Brook and they moved cautiously along the mud-churned path.

A stone walled building stood to one side. On the other side, there was fencing, and behind the fencing, a bull was blotting out the sun. He snorted, pawed the dust and rolled his eyes in their direction.

"Got nothing better to do?" Duncan pulled a face that said, "Bull - you don't bother me."

"I hope the fencing holds for our sakes," Guffrey noted.

Edgar pointed up beyond the milking shed. "I should think that leads to the back of the farm."

They passed several sheds and a barn and at the very back near a wall, they found a small, ivy covered, ramshackled hut.

"Is there anybody here?" Edgar called. "Anyone about….."

"Did someone call?" An elderly gnome poked his head through a loop of ivy.

"What a sight!" he thought. "Six young gnomes, thin and shabby all looking like they've seen a ghost or …" And he said aloud -"You look like you've been through hell."

"We have," was all they said.

The elderly gnome pulled back the ivy like a curtain.

"Come inside. Please be seated."

They entered into the dark interior and sat down

on straw seats.

"You must have food and drink and rest. Then perhaps you can tell me what happened to you. Ted where are you? We have visitors."

Both Gromley and Ted were generous and kind and fussed about. A meal was hastily prepared of mashed pumpkin seeds and cabbage soup. They soon felt better, but they would not rest.

"There are too many bad things going on," said Edgar, and one by one they gave their story - who they were, where they came from, how they had been abducted, drugged and forced to work underground. They told them the horrors of the murders and Knobby's plans to poison the reservoir with fermented roots.

The old gnomes listened in silence. Gromley, stood with his shoulders hunched; his thumbs hooked within his bracers. He frowned the whole while, and Ted, grim with shock and sadness cast his grey eyes about the group.

"But now you must rest," Gromley said at last. "We will make sure your families are told that you are here and safe. I recall the name Knobby. He was at a meeting a while back. Yes, I remember he spoke about the big folk. He believed they wanted to destroy the little folk."

Now the truth was out and the young gnomes, exhausted and relieved, lay down to rest and were soon asleep.

Later Gromley spoke with Ted.

"We must ask the fairies to take messages to the families, and ask them, where possible, to come here. We need to stop this Knobby - he must be arrested and tried by the Council of the Little People for the abduction of the gnomes, and the murder of Lord and Lady Flanelle. Ted will you ask your nephew, Warner, if he can bring the fairies here and stress the urgency."

"He'll be in the back field." Ted went off to find his nephew.

Soon a band of fairies flew off to find the families. Within a few days, they returned with, what seemed like, a small army of gnomes following behind.

I must explain something - in the fairy world there are more men gnomes than women gnomes, (just as there are more girl fairies than boy fairies), but should a gnome marry and have children, the children rarely arrive one at a time, they usually arrive four or five at once. Male gnomes tend to make wonderful fathers and wonderful uncles too, and unbeknown to Brook he was now a father of four young children, and when they suddenly appeared with Rosy, helped by several brothers, and all the children started calling out to him "Daddy, Daddy," Brook was overwhelmed.

The McNezzar brothers too were overjoyed to find the youngest of them safe, and they hugged him and he hugged them back. Then there were bakers arriving with food - I might add, and several fishermen, a carpenter and a blacksmith. And everyone was overjoyed.

Early next morning the gnomes were ready, and they set off towards the reservoir. Only the elderly gnomes and Rosy with her little ones, stayed behind.

It took Giles nearly a week of walking, but finally he arrived at a big blue house on a hill where he believed the miners lived.

Burley Bill answered the doorbell and he thought

his luck was back. A goblin was standing at the door. But what was the little fellow stammering about?

"Lord and Lady Flanelle are dead." Giles was throwing up his arms.

"Come with me young man," Burley Bill invited.

The goblin followed in through to a dark hallway, up a flight of stairs, across a landing and into an enormous sitting room where a large bay window held views across the valley.

"Bailey - see what I have here - another goblin like the other two."

Bailey walked over to Burley Bill, and when he saw the goblin, his eyes glinted greedily. He smiled and revealed a golden tooth.

"Come where we can see you," said Bailey and he lifted Giles onto a table in the centre of the room.

Burley Bill found a map and unrolled it before Giles. But soon the big folk were disappointed, for instead of pointing to a spot on the map where gold might be found the little man was jumping up and down and yelling at them, and it was quite clear that this goblin had no intention of showing them where to find gold. And that was when Burley Bill and Bailey started getting nasty.

"Some believe that, by dangling a goblin by his tail over a map, he will point to the spot where gold can be found."

"Goblins don't have tails. I think you've got that

wrong. What about dangling him by his foot out of the window, or over a pan of boiling water," suggested Bailey.

Now Giles realized his mistake. He shuffled backwards. His eyes darted round the room, and he clasped his clammy hands together. How to make a quick exit?

"I do know," began the goblin, his eyes bulging, "where gold is …b buried," and he pointed to the window. "There in caves beside the reservoir. Can I go now?"

"No," Bailey said. "You can show us."

Back at the caves, Knobby had been planning, for now he had a new vision. Once he had thought himself a common goblin, but after the meeting with the Lord and Lady Flanelle in their plush apartment, he had felt the stirrings of jealousy and greed, and when he took a handful of the gold dust and let it filter through his fingers, he knew himself to be - almost regal. It was all going to his head. And this is how he saw it: - in order to recruit workers he would have to impress with a show of wealth. His mighty wheelbarrow (very small to you or me) could be turned around and hitched to a sleek black rat, like a chariot of old. And he would give a speech:

"We shall push the big folk back and be great once again. No more will they walk tall across our pastures and consume our land. I have the way, I have the will, and now I have the gold dust and if you follow me I will reward you all, as my loyal band of goblins."

He was practising this speech in his head as he climbed up out of the cave from the exit hole on the eastern side of the hill that faced the reservoir. Bright light hit his face. He squinted, and then gazed over to one side where a road ran down from the Western Hills. A large, shiny, coffee coloured car was moving rapidly towards the hidden caves, and in an instant Knobby saw Burley Bill seated at the wheel; Bailey in the passenger's seat and, standing on the dashboard, Giles pointing up towards him.

Knobby gasped in horror, "It's Giles the traitor, the informer, with his big folk friends to take revenge on me."

Knobby moved back inside the cave and hurriedly

rolled the round exit stone across the hole.

The car parked beside the reservoir and two big folk stepped out and walked purposely towards the hill.

"Can't see no caves," said Bailey studying the hill before him. "Go get the goblin."

"You get him."

They returned to the car. Burley Bill opened up the door and grabbed the goblin like a ball. "Where are they - these caves?"

"Up," Giles pointed his sucker finger. "There - there are three large boulders like a triangle set into the hill about half way up. Push the top one to the left."

They dropped the goblin back inside car and set off again, but in their haste, forgot to lock the doors. Giles slipped out and this time he skirted round the reservoir and travelled east.

The two big folk scrambled half way up the hill and hunted round. "There ain't no boulders," said Bailey kicking at the earth. "What's this? Three stones set in a triangle." He grabbed the top stone and threw it down the hill.

"Yes, there is a kind of cave," said Bailey poking his finger through the hole.

"Go get the shovels."

"You get them."

They both returned to the car.

"Oh no you left the door unlocked."

"Me?"

"That blasted goblin he's gone. Oh what the heck? Get the shovels and start digging."

As the two big folk were climbing up the hillside with their shovels, the gnomes, armed with spears and catapults, were in the valley just a short distance from the caves.

Knobby could hear the big folk talking. He scurried down the inner wall to the cave floor. Then moving round in darkness he stumbled upon something furry, something horrible - something hard and smelly - the dead rat.

"I'll get a torch." He found one in its holder, lit it and looked around. It seemed there were bodies everywhere.

Knobby considered his options. He only knew of

two ways to leave the cave: - the entrance hole above and through the water channel. "They won't get me. I'm too clever for them."

He moved towards the pool, placed his hands into the water and felt around to find a metal hook. A chain connected to the hook hung straight down and disappeared into blackness. Knobby tugged the chain once. "Dong" it sounded underwater. Then he pulled it once again. "Dong" and after several a moments a pink whiskered fish rose from beneath the surface of the water.

"Just checking you're still there. I have a job for you my friend, but first I need my luggage."

His luggage consisted of a dagger and several sacks of gold dust. He set to work. On his first trip to the storeroom, he found an empty barrel into which he placed a harness for the fish, ropes and twine. He rolled this barrel along the corridor to the pool. On his second trip, he found another barrel. This one was not empty - it contained several sacks of gold dust, and now he rolled this second barrel back along the corridor.

Now all he had to do was make a fuse. He took

the twine and greased it like a taper. (Do not ask where he got the grease from - perhaps the rat served the purpose.) Then he returned to the storeroom and walked towards the chamber where the vat was kept. He turned the door handle and pushed inside. With one hand across his face and crawling sideways like a crab, Knobby moved over to the vat. Then he placed one end of the greasy twine on the ground and hastily retreated. All the while he was unraveling the ball of twine. At the pool he dropped it to the ground near the waters' edge. Now the fuse was set.

Knobby took hold the underwater chain and tugged - "Dong" the bell rang out beneath, "Dong" and once again the catfish surfaced.

"Good girl." He harnessed up the fish and attached the ropes, first to the heavy barrel containing several sacks of gold dust, then to the other barrel, containing just his dagger. Soon, he told himself; he would climb inside this barrel, and close the lid. The catfish would then pull the barrels through the water tunnel and out to safety. Knobby took the flaming torch dropped it to the ground and lit the fuse.

The fuse was burning nicely. He watched it for a moment as the flame crept along the ground, and then he stepped back and back and back, and he fell into darkness - and she was on to him, with beating wings, clawing at his eyes, tearing at his face. Her own face, beautiful with oriental eyes, her wings - silk black, not quite a butterfly, not quite a fairy, and Knobby suffocated and died, and Pricilla too - she died.

And in an instant, the catfish fled, dragging two barrels - one full of gold dust and the other with a single dagger.

And in another instant a flash, a bang, and outside in the valley the gnomes saw the flash, heard the explosion and watched as mist rose high into the air like a smoking volcano. It smelt distinctly bad.

"Like the evil brew," thought the gnomes.

On the other side of the hill, two big folk had shot out, flown skyward and landed in the reservoir. And Giles the goblin, running beside the reservoir, kept on running.

Edgar finished his story, although he was unaware

of the role played by Pricilla.

"So, was that the end of it?" asked Dominic. "There was no great battle with pitchforks - just puff - everything went up in smoke."

"No, no great battle with the pitchforks." said Edgar. "Knobby was never seen again. We believed he died in the explosion. Another time I will tell you what happened next."

"Night," said Edgar and the little folk went to bed.

The "Good" Fairies

"It's raining," said Cora looking out the window. "I'm not staying in."

"If you are going out - bring us back some water. I'm sure you'll find something to carry it in," said Elzamere.

"There's plenty of water out there," observed Roly Poly.

The fairies ventured out. "Yes," said Estine, staring at the ever-growing puddles that were forming on the pavement, "there's no shortage of water."

"Have you ever tried puddle skipping?" Roly Poly asked. "It's like throwing a pebble so that it skims across the water. You take a low running leap towards a puddle, then just before the edge, a slow sloping hop, keep your feet tight together and you bounce across the water to the other side. I've seen it done."

"And can you do it?" asked Cora, "I'd like to see that."

"Yes," said Bella. They were keen to see a belly flop.

"No, not today…too much air turbulence."

"Air turbulence?"

"Yes, too much."

"My feet are wet." Cora moaned.

Just then, a car rolled down the narrow lane towards them. It hit a puddle in the gutter and sent a spray of water up and over and they were drenched.

"Now my hair is flat," said Cora with a pout.

"Let's go over there, beneath that porch," suggested Poppy. They flew over and huddled in a covered doorway. A grey cat with yellow eyes raced across the road and sat beside them, with the same idea so it seemed, of sheltering from the rain. Now, quite perversely, he began to wash himself.

"Aren't you wet enough?" asked Roly Poly.

The cat stopped and for a moment he gazed around. Had he heard something, seen something? He swished his tail. But the cat saw nothing and continued with his washing. Suddenly the front door opened.

"There you are Archie? In you come." Archie jumped neatly up the step and through the door. The man standing in the hallway held the door ajar.

"Are we invited in?" thought the fairies and they too stepped inside.

However, the man was merely leaving, and he called to someone up the stairs. "I'm off. See you at 7.00. Take care." He left the house and closed the door behind him.

Archie the cat walked pertly through the hall into a kitchen and the fairies followed in behind. It was a large, long and tidy kitchen with a log burning fire at one end. Archie and the fairies sat down before the fire.

Some several minutes later Dominic spoke out. "I think I'm nearly dry."

"Me too," said Estine. "It's cosy here. See the cat's asleep."

"Perhaps he had a late night on the tiles," Cora mused.

Then they heard noises: - a door was opening, stairs were creaking, footsteps, and a woman walked through the kitchen door. She held her dressing gown wrapped tight around her waist. She sighed, rubbed her brow and walked across the room. She took a glass from a cupboard, moved towards the sink, turned the tap and filled the glass with water. Archie woke to see his owner by the sink. He meowed, padded over and tried to wind his furry body round her slippered feet.

"Oh where are my pills?" she said, "and John has left for work. I'll call Mandy." She took her phone that was lying on the worktop and tried a number. "No signal. It must be the weather."

The cat meowed.

"Oh Archie, I'm too tired to cuddle you. I am going back to bed."

"Poor lady," thought the fairies. "Is she ill?" and "Poor Archie, has he been fed?"

The cat sat on the mat - disappointed, and the woman left the kitchen.

"I'm going to follow her and see if she's okay," said Ivy, then she, Poppy and Estine flew off.

"I think someone forgot to feed the cat." Dominic gazed about. "There's no food in his bowl, just a little water."

"Let's find the cat food and feed him," suggested Roly Poly.

The fairies opened all the cupboards and hunted

round for cat food. Roly Poly found a box beneath the sink.

"This box has a picture of a cat on it. Looks like biscuits, could be cat biscuits," he sniffed the contents. "I'm not really sure what it smells of." He turned to Dominic, "Help me pour some out."

They lifted up the box, tipped it, and filled the bowl well beyond its rim and the overflow scattered on the floor.

"Better too much than too little. Come on Archie," said Cora. But Archie turned away and left the kitchen.

"A very perverse cat," said Roly Poly.

"Yes, very perverse," Bella agreed. "Let's find the others."

Upstairs the woman was lying in the bed with Archie on the covers rolled against her feet.

"I wish I'd brought my phone upstairs," the woman said, talking to herself, or may be to the cat.

"I'm just too tired to go down again. And a nice cup of sweet tea, I could do with that," she sighed. Then she leaned back against the pillow and closed her eyes.

"Come on," said Ivy, "one sweet tea, one phone. That's not too tall an order."

"Well it could be for fairies," said Roly Poly.

The kettle was half-full and they switched it on. Then they found a mug, a tea bag, milk and sugar, and a tray.

How many fairies does it take to make one cup of tea? Depends on the weight of the kettle, but they managed. So, one mug of sweet tea and one mobile phone were carried to the bedroom.

Archie sat up and stared at the tea tray as it came floating round the room and landed on a bedside table.

'Meow,' was just enough to wake the woman.

"Tea, lovely, and my phone," she said. "I don't remember going down the stairs - how strange." She tried the phone again - still no signal and she sipped her tea.

"I'm feeling hungry now. A cheese and tomato sandwich would be nice. No hurry," then she rested back against the pillow, "yes that would be nice."

"Are you sure she can't see us?" asked Dominic as they flew down the stairs. "Anyway, Roly Poly - one sandwich - one cheese and tomato sandwich."

"Yes chef."

They found a tomato, some cheese, bread and butter, a knife and a plate. The tomato was soft and the pips popped out when they tried to cut it. The bread and cheese were crumbly and the butter hard. They left a bit of a mess, but they placed the sandwich on a plate and carried it up the stairs.

Now Archie saw the plate floating through the air. This too landed on the table. Once again, a single 'meow' was enough to rouse the woman.

"A sandwich - how strange. I don't remember making it." She took a bite. "Just right." Then she tried the phone again.

"John I have run out of pills. Can you bring some on your way home? No need to hurry back. See you, love."

The fairies returned to the kitchen.

"What good fairies we are," Estine reflected. "But if we were really good, we would clear the mess up."

"Yes," said Roly Poly, "and we would not be looking at that pot of peanut butter, up there in the cupboard, just above the sugar, and thinking to ourselves: - 'there's not much left, perhaps just enough for eight fairies.'"

"Do you think we can unscrew the lid?" asked Piper.

"Of course, I've done this before - get the teaspoons."

When they finished eating, they left the teaspoons (more like shovels to the fairies) on the draining board.

"We'll take the empty jar," suggested Dominic, "Elzamere wants us to bring some water back."

They left the house through the cat flap.

"I have an idea," said Dominic as they flew towards the thatch, "if we place the empty jar on the roof - on that flat bit, we can leave it there and have a fresh supply of rainwater."

So they all flew up and placed the jar squarely on roof.

"Yes, that will work and Elzamere will be pleased," and just then, they realised, that was what they wanted - to please Elzamere.

At 7 O'clock, John returned home.

"I'm back - brought your pills." He wandered through into the kitchen. The cat was sitting by his bowl, looking very hungry, and the bowl was overflowing with cat litter.

"How strange."

All the cupboard doors were open. There were dribbles of milk and water on the worktops, and cheese crumbs, breadcrumbs, tomato pips and butter smudges everywhere.

"Bit of a mess," he thought, "not like Celia at all." Then he saw eight teaspoons on the draining board - "Strange."

"Hello love," said Celia. She was standing at the kitchen door. "I feel much better now."

"We didn't go far," Ivy told Elzamere, "there was too much air turbulence."

"Turbulence?" queried Elzamere.

"Yes," said Bella, flicking back her orange plait, "too much."

"We went a few doors up - met a cat and helped a lady." And the fairies told Elzamere the story of their day.

Later in the evening, Elzamere remarked, "From Edgar's tale it's clear that sometimes the big folk can see the little folk, and I too know this to be true."

The fairies were sitting round and were keen to listen to the elf.

Sophie and George

"Sometimes the big folk do see the little folk. When I was young, I lived in a thatched roof, much like this one here. An old lady owned the cottage. I remember her garden. It was lovely with its daffodils and tulips in the spring and in the summer, rambling roses, lupines and hollyhocks. The old woman would potter round her garden, and I would often watch as she pruned; watered plants; filled the bird feeder and even talked to the birds. Then one day, as the lady stooped to pull a weed she caught sight of me sitting by a tree - and she smiled - no more surprised than if she'd seen a robin. I smiled back. She told me her name was Sophie. I said that I was Elzamere the elf, and I was living in her roof.

I was invited in to have tea with her. I remember Sophie had blue eyes that twinkled, grey wavy hair, and a soft smile. We became friends. It may seem odd, but we had much in common - for one thing, we were both old fashioned. She seemed very fond of me, and she taught me things, and took pleasure in it.

'I'll show you how to make pastry.' She measured

out some butter, sifted flour into a bowl and stirred it with a wooden spoon. I copied using my own bowl, which was really just a small teacup. Sophie waved her wooden spoon like a wand, and indeed, it seemed her pastry was magic. She made pies, and cakes - even fairy cakes.

'Why not elf cakes?' I asked.

Then she taught me how to sew and knit. We would often sit in her parlour by the coal fire, drinking tea; she, from a large china cup, and I, from a china thimble and she would tell me stories from her childhood. She could remember her grandmother. This Victorian woman wore black clothes and a small white cap and was very strict. She would box her children's ears, which was a common custom in those days. Sophie said she was frightened of her grandmother, but she loved her mother dearly.

I remember one evening we were knitting - she with huge wooden needles and me with two hatpins - I was making an egg cosy for Sophie and she looked over approvingly.

'You learn very quickly.'

Sophie told me that when she was young she had

wanted to be a teacher. 'But my parents could not afford for me to be trained. I had won a scholarship at school, but they needed me to go to work and make some money. Even if I had become a teacher, if ever I chose to marry, I would lose my job. In those days, only unmarried women were allowed to teach. Instead, I went into service, meaning I was a servant at one of the big houses. I worked very hard as we all did, polishing and cleaning, fetching and carrying. It was one of my jobs to fetch the milk. I would take a large metal jug and collect milk from the milk cart. That is when I met George, the milkman. I remember he had brown eyes, a mop of red hair and cheeky grin, and soon we were a courting couple and a very handsome couple too,' said Sophie, her blue eyes twinkling.

'Every Friday night I went to George's family home, and had sausages for tea. There were eight brothers and sisters. I still remember their names,' and she ran though a list of names in her head.

'I remember I had to sit on an orange box - they were very poor, but to me it was all laughter and fun. Every Sunday after church, George and I would walk down to the stream and talk. We would sit on the grass near the water beneath the willow tree and watch the ferryman with his little boat take people from one side of the water to the other.

One Sunday I remember it was quiet and hot. I was wearing my best dress. It was blue, as blue as the sky on that sunny day, and I wore a wide brimmed hat trimmed with ribbons. George was so handsome in his Sunday best. It seemed to me everything was happiness and it would last forever.

Then suddenly George whispered - 'There - there's a kingfisher on that branch.' I held my breath. A brilliant flash of blue and orange, a glimpse of beauty, but in a moment the kingfisher was gone.

In the following year, it seemed to me, just like the kingfisher, our happiness was gone. War was declared. Terrible rumours spread as to what might happen if we were to lose the war. They said it would be a war to end all wars, and very soon, George enlisted. Before he left, he said to me, 'If you will have me, when I return, we will marry.'

And I said, 'Yes, I will marry you.'

He took out a clean white handkerchief from his

pocket, opened it up and showed me a little brooch like a china rose, and gave to me as a present.

We said goodbye and he went away to war, but like many a young man in that war, he did not return, and I never married.'

Now I felt so sad for Sophie, for suddenly, she looked like a very old lady. Of course, there was a lot more life story for Sophie, as she told me over many an evening. She had worked in a sweet shop, in a bakery, she had become a manageress and later she worked in offices, and she had friends and happy stories too, but of course, the story that remained with me was her sad love story.

Sometimes her nephew, Niles, would come to visit at the cottage and bring his wife Lottie and their child. He was an abrupt man. He could not see me, but in any case, I usually stayed away when he came around. But one day, I was in the garden and their child Henry came trotting over. He pointed his chubby little hand at me as if to say, 'I see you,' but his parents sitting on the garden bench saw nothing.

'Over here Henry - don't scratch yourself on those rose bushes.' He lowered his voice, 'If this were my garden I would pull those roses out - what a mess they make when all the petals fall.'

Sophie was in the house rattling cups and saucers and putting biscuits on a tray. 'I'll be out in a minute,' she said. 'You all take sugar?'

'No Aunt Sophie,' her nephew tapped his slim belly. 'That was some time ago. No sugar please.' He turned to his wife, 'I think she is getting past it. Did you know the neighbours say she's always talking to herself - in the garden, in the kitchen? One said they heard her calling out for Elsie while staring at the roof.'

'Yes,' replied his wife, 'and she forgets: - people's names, what day it is, her keys, her glasses, and she is always leaving windows open, turning things off when they should be on and on when they should be off. It could be dangerous. This place might go up in smoke. Can you imagine if that thatch caught light?'

He stared upwards at the thatch. 'What an expense to keep this place,' he said. 'I couldn't do it. Much better to sell.'

A few weeks later Sophie's nephew came to the

cottage.

'Come on Auntie you will be much happier in the home. Bring your stick. I'll carry your bags and we'll sort all your things for you.'

'What about Elzamere?' she said looking straight at me sitting on a cushion in the corner.

'Yes that's right, this way,' and he took Sophie slowly to the door.

I returned to the thatch roof, sat alone, and felt very sad.

Some weeks later Niles returned and stood outside by the front door. Then a car pulled up and a man in a suit carrying a bundle of papers emerged from the car. Of course, I went down to see what was happening. I might hear news of Sophie I thought. The two men shook hands and started talking about the weather. The wind had picked up and the bundle of papers started flapping about.

'We had better go inside.' Niles opened the front door. I followed in behind.

'So sorry to hear the sad news,' said the man with the bundle of papers.

'Yes,' replied Niles, 'it was only last month when

Aunt Sophie went into the home. I cannot believe it, and now she is dead. She was a good age. She had a good life and did not suffer at the end. To be honest we really don't know why she died. Old age I suppose.'

I heard no more. I found a dark corner in the parlour and sat down to weep. Sometime later I heard the two men leave the cottage. Finally, I stood up. I was a strong elf even then, and was ready to leave the cottage for the last time, but for a moment I hesitated, something caught my eye, beside the old clock, on the mantelpiece, I saw a china brooch. It was pink and shaped like a rose. I had never seen it before, but I knew exactly what it was. I took it down. It was rather large for me to carry, but I did.

I thought, 'I will find somewhere to place this in memory of Sophie.'

Well where do you suppose I went? I went to the church and there, followed a path down towards the stream.

'Here beneath this willow tree,' I thought, 'this is where Sophie and George once sat and watched the ferryman as he carried folk from one side of the water to the other.'

There was a little boat in a jetty - not a ferry but someone else's little boat. No one was about. I sat down and placed the brooch on the ground beside me. Where could I leave it safely? Perhaps, hidden in the knotted roots of the willow tree? I sat for a while and watched as yellow leaves glided across the stream, and then I turned to where I had placed the brooch - but now it was gone.

'Where?'

I stood up and looked about, and there across on the other side of the water I saw two fairies watching me. For a moment I thought - 'Have they stolen it?' But no, I realised they had no china brooch.

The man fairy had a mop of red hair and a cheeky grin. He had brilliant orange and blue wings the colour of a Kingfisher. The lady had dark blond, wavy hair, eyes that twinkled and a soft smile. Her wings were blue, as blue as the sky, and on her pale blue dress she wore a small pink rose. In an instant they were gone."

The little folk had been listening quietly to the story and for a few moments and no one spoke.

At last Cora said, "Well that was a very sad story, very sad, but the ending was nice."

Little Ivy looked tearful.

Dominic asked. "You know - when we listen to stories about the big folk, do they tell stories about us - I mean tell stories about the fairy folk."

"Yes," said Edgar - "they tell fairy stories. They were very popular in the Victorian age."

"That was when Sophie's grandmother boxed her children's ears?" Poppy pulled a face, as much to say, "I would not like that time."

Cora turned to Roly Poly, "If I play the part of Sophie with her blue wings, will you be George - the King Fisher Fairy?"

"No, I'd rather play the part of Guffrey. Would you like to play the rat?"

"No," said Cora indignantly.

"And what happened?" Dominic looked at Edgar, "after the explosion on the hill. Were there any more bad Goblins?"

"Tomorrow," said Edgar. "I'll tell you tomorrow evening."

When the time came the little folk were busy trying to create things out of straw.

"What's that?" Bella asked looking over at Roly Poly.

"It's a bookcase, maybe or a place for putting shoes, or anything, just a piece of furniture, or may be a foot rest."

"I see," said Bella doubtfully.

"This reminds me of when I used to live in the thatch before - everything was made of straw," said Elzamere. "It's like straw hats - they are fine, but just now I'd rather have a woollen cap."

Piper looked up at Edgar. "You were going to tell us about what happened next - after the hill blew up."

Edgar sat forward. He raised his hand against his eyebrows. "Yes, yes," he said, remembering.

The Great Adventure Continues

"We were in the valley, all of us with our spears and catapults while the strange mist and smoke and evil smell was rising from the hill. We decided not to climb up, but to take a route around the hill towards the reservoir.

What we saw on the other side surprised us. Two big folk, fully clothed were splashing about in the water. Puffing and panting, they struggled to the waters' edge and crawled out. One started wringing out his shirt ends, the other searched his pockets. Then, I remember clearly the sound of their boots squelching as they walked towards their car. Both were very angry and cursing loudly. They unlocked the car, climbed inside, slammed the doors and sped off towards the hills.

We turned again and now we noticed a wooden barrel floating in the water. Remembering what Guffrey had said about using barrels to bring goods to the caves, we decided to investigate. We quickly made a raft from twigs, and with dock leaves for oars, Guffrey and I paddled over to the barrel. We grabbed the barrel and tried to tow it back. But it would not move.

'It seems it's anchored down,' Guffrey pointed, 'look, there's a rope attached. Let see if we can lift the anchor.'

The two of us took hold of the rope and pulled, but instead of bringing up the anchor, we pulled a monster from the depths, or so it seemed. She had large pink glazed eyes and silver bristles. She was clearly saying 'Oh!' as if disturbed and was blowing bubbles in the water.

'The catfish,' said Guffrey. The two of us slipped into the water and carefully undid the harness, and once freed the fish swam away. We towed the barrel back to the side, lifted it from the water and placed it with the harness on ground. Now we noticed there were two ropes attached to the harness, so we guessed there was yet another barrel in the water. We hauled the other in. This second one was extremely heavy, and it took several of us to lift it out. We flipped off the lids and looked inside. The first barrel was empty, but for a single dagger. The second held several sacks of gold dust. Clearly, something had gone wrong for Knobby. If he had escaped, he would have taken the sacks and the dagger with him.

Now we could all return home. We placed half the sacks into the other barrel, to make the load lighter, and took turns to roll them back towards the farm.

What a welcome awaited us when we arrived just a few days later. Gromley and Ted were greatly relieved to see us safe and sound and Rosy and the little ones were thrilled. The old gentlemen invited us to stay a while, and I remember we had a celebration. The cooks prepared the meal. No more horrible gruel - but turnip puffs with rosemary and thyme, spiced cabbage rolls, tomato pickle pies, hazel nuts, apple pudding and acorn cups of honeyed ale. We had our fill and more. We gnomes do like our food and drink. Then Jasper led the singing. We sang old songs and danced. The little ones joined in with giggles and handstands on the grass.

Soon my brothers would return to their garden life, and the others to their homes. 'But', I said, 'I have changed and I want to see more of the world,' and they all agreed I had changed. And now I had new friends - Jasper, Robin, Guffrey, Duncan and Brook and his lovely wife.

For a while, we were the six heroes, and as we told our tales, I admit we did exaggerate just a bit.

'The rat like a dragon,' said Guffrey, 'was roaring with a breath of fire. I took the spear, and cut him down to size.'

The little ones and fairies were listening with open mouths, in fear and admiration.

'And,' said Duncan, 'we climbed the cave walls that rose like mighty mountains, and as we jumped from rock to rock we saw beneath, may be, thirty goblins, waving clubs and crawling up towards us, but Guffrey here, he cast his net and caught the goblins all tangled in the net, and they flapped like fish and fell into the deep darkness of the cave.'

Gromley, Ted, and all the little folk were undecided as to what to do with the gold dust. But as you know, there is a saying amongst the little folk that 'all dust belongs to the wind,' and as it turned out the wind wanted a say in the matter.

After the party, we all found somewhere to bed down. I found a corner, just outside the shed. Now you might say it was the drink, but I distinctly heard someone was calling.

'Edgar' a wind was calling me. 'Edgar you take that sack of gold, open it and throw it all to me,' she said. It was definitely a 'she' as an image was appearing, and what an image. She was very tall, as tall as the big folk, and beautiful, with dark eyes and lashes and long streaming copper coloured hair, and her dress had garnets shaped like serpent scales and was edged with silver feathers. I did nothing I simply stared. 'Now are you listening?' she said, and I was smitten.

I stood up and several saw me walk over to the sacks. I opened one and cast the contents to the wind.

'All dust belongs to the wind,' I said in something of a trance. Now the beautiful wind caught the gold dust in her cupped hands and blew a kiss to me and some gold dust caught my eyes.

'Are you mad?' said the lads. They saw nothing of the wind, but fearing I would throw away another sack of gold dust, they sat on me. I did not struggle, for my part, all I saw was sunshine.

Over the next few days, they seemed to think I was in some kind of sleep and tried to wake me, but all I did was smile and watch the sunshine in my eyes.

'Too much ale,' said Gromley.

'Too much stress,' said Rosy

But a fairy called Jasmine understood the problem.

'Gold dust in the eyes,' she said. 'You should make him cry.'

'Let's try a sad song,' said Jasper, and he sang:

'We met beneath the blossomed bough
And before the blossom fell
I sang to you of love,
Cristy, Cristy, Oh Cristobel
You're the love within my breast
Like the dew upon the flower.

And through the summer days
Beneath a cloudless blue,
We walked upon the heather
And pledged our love and life
and happiness together.
Oh Cristy, Cristy, Cristobel
You're the love within my breast.
Like the dew upon the flower.

And in the gold of autumn,
beneath the russet trees,
I sang my song, still sweet upon the breeze.
Cristy, Cristy, Oh Cristobel
You are all and everything to me.

Yet so cruel the winter day,
In the snow shadows of the bough,
I cried and fell -
Cristobel don't leave me, don't die,
But my sweet, my brave, my Cristobel.
Passed away that day.

And now in the blossoming of spring,
my love,
As swallows fly high above the bough,
I know they hear me sing
Cristy, Cristy, my lovely Cristobel.
You're the love within my breast
And the dew upon the flower.'

After Jasper finished his song, it seemed everyone was crying except for me. I had heard the words and still I saw only sunshine.

'It's no good,' they all agreed, 'we should dunk him in the duck pond. That will clear his eyesight.'

They lifted me bodily, carried me to the pond and dropped me in. My head sank beneath water, but I closed my eyes and still I saw the orb of golden light. My head popped up and I grinned in the same half-witted fashion. Now I remember I could just see through the glow of light. They were standing on the edge, throwing up their arms and arguing, and somehow it all seemed very funny to me. I dragged myself out and sat down to watch. They did not see me, and they did not see me laugh when a huge gust of wind (I believe she was laughing too) blew the whole lot of them right into the pond. But laugh I did and I laughed until the tears were rolling down my cheeks, and suddenly the ball of light was gone, and I could see quite clearly.

After some discussion, we decided to hold the gold dust for the benefit of fairies. We have so much to thank them for and fairies are the closest to the winds. Much later, I put a portion of the gold dust in the rainbow pot. It must still be buried somewhere deep beneath the fallen tree."

"You have a strange relationship with the winds," Elzamere remarked.

"Yes, they are a capricious lot. Much like the best of elves."

"Did all the bad goblins die in the explosion?"

asked Dominic.

"No, there was Grimweed and Stark and Walter - that's another story for another night."

"I'm thinking," said Elzamere, "I would like some wool, a beetroot, and a large bowl." She said it like someone listing shopping. "Tomorrow will be soon enough. Night," she yawned and went to bed.

Some Wool, a Beetroot and a Hunting Sheep

Next morning Elzamere requested, "Maybe someone will be kind enough to gather strands of wool off the barbed wire fencing from the sheep's grazing fields."

"It could be dangerous," said Roly Poly sounding serious. "I've seen huge hunting sheep."

"I'm not afraid of hunting sheep," said Piper bravely.

"What do they eat?" asked Cora.

"Yes what do they hunt?" asked Poppy.

"Almost anything," replied Roly Poly coolly.

"Let's be clear," Dominic explained, "They're just ordinary sheep. There's no such thing as hunting sheep."

"Of course not," said Bella, "there's no such thing."

Roly Poly laughed, "Everybody knows that."

Piper looked abashed.

"We knew that," said Cora

"Yes, we knew that," said Poppy.

"So you three will collect the wool and bring it back?" She turned to Dominic, Roly Poly and Bella. "You'll need to find some sharp chipped pebbles to cut away the wool."

"Yes" they said and off they flew.

"And who will find a beetroot for me?"

Little Ivy raised her hand. "Me I know what they look like. They are purple and grow in the soil."

Poppy, Cora and Piper offered to go as well.

Now there was only Estine left. "Would you like to come with us?" Elzamere offered. "I want to visit Bead and Silk. Edgar's coming too."

Ivy and her group set off to find a beetroot.

"We are bound to find one," Poppy was sure, "with so many gardeners in the village."

They searched the cottage gardens. There were cabbages in rows, runner beans on canes, carrots, giant marrows, tomato plants, peppers, peas and all else besides, but no beetroots.

"Let's try the allotments," suggested Cora.

They headed off towards the outskirts of the village and hovered just above the fencing that enclosed the allotments.

"It's very quiet," Poppy observed, "just one man and his dog. Let's go in."

They flew across the crops and landed on a water butt.

Now the man was strolling through his plot talking to his collie dog. "I'll have salad tonight."

"What is he saying?" Cora asked the others.

"He's having salad tonight," Ivy repeated.

"Nice…"

The old man trotted down between the lines of produce. He picked some lettuce leaves, a small cucumber and a large ripe tomato and placed them in a box.

"A beetroot, I think." He took his hand fork, dug down a little way and eased a beetroot from the ground.

"Splendid," he said studying his prize beet, and with his pocket-knife he cut away the muddy roots and leaves.

"Come on Robbie," he said turning to his dog. He moved back along the path, placed the box on the ground and settled in his deckchair.

"My glasses, where are they?" Fumbling in his

pocket, he found his reading glasses, set them on his nose and opened up his newspaper.

"Um, uhem uh," he mumbled to himself. His dog, beside him on the grass, was dozing in the midday sun.

Now the fairies flew across the plot and searched around looking for another beetroot.

"This will do," said Poppy.

Each took a leaf and pulled, and pulled, but nothing budged.

"It's hopeless." Ivy shrugged her shoulders like a tiny wrestler. She felt tightness in her muscles after pulling at the leaf. "We'll have to take that beetroot in the box. The man is busy reading and the dog is fast asleep. What's to stop us?"

Poppy, Cora, and Piper stared at Ivy. "Is this Ivy speaking?" but then they simply said, "Okay."

Ivy led the way, followed by Cora, Poppy and Piper. The dog was snoring quietly. All well so far. The fairies flew up and over into the box. They took hold of the "prize" and lifted it above their heads like a trophy. Carefully they stepped up and out the box. At this point, Cora tripped and lost her grip, and the others, now stumbling out of step, dropped the beetroot. It rolled away down the path. The collie roused by a "plump, plop" sound saw the beetroot rolling like ball and in a moment, he was running after it. He snatched it, rolled it, licked it, chewed it and dropped it in the ditch, and with red beetroot juice, foaming on his mouth ran back towards his owner.

"Robbie," said the man, "you dopey dog, that was for my tea. Now I'll have to find another one. I'm really angry with you." But he did not sound angry. Perhaps he was too good-natured to be angry at his dog.

He stood up and once again took his hand fork. Soon he returned with another beetroot. He sat back down, took out a sandwich box, and started on his lunch.

The fairies went over to the beetroot lying in the ditch.

"Yes," said Poppy with authority, "It has teeth marks, the juice is bleeding out, but I think it will do. We should wait until the dog's asleep, before we take it home."

They sat down beneath a leaf and waited. Twiddling with her spiky hair Cora sighed deeply. She was bored. "We could see how the others are getting on and come back later. The sheep farm's over there."

They set off, but just beyond the fencing, they came face to face with the other fairies who were heading back towards the village.

"You look pleased with yourselves," said Cora, and they did - they looked quite smug.

"We had to move a herd of sheep to get this load."

And what a load - the heavy wool was stuffed inside their waistcoats, their pockets, and wrapped around their necks.

"We did really well," said Roly Poly proudly. "And have you got your beetroot? I bet not."

"Well, not yet but we met a hunting sheep," Cora chimed in.

"I told you hunting sheep don't exist." Dominic sounded almost cross. Bella laughed behind her hands. Roly Poly laughed outright.

"Well seeing is believing. Come and see."

So Dominic, Roly Poly and Bella peered above the

fencing.

"Look there," Cora pointed to the collie. He was certainly the same colour as a sheep. He was big and fluffy and from where they stood, yes he did look something like a sheep, and when he raised his face, it was clear, his mouth was stained with blood, (or I should say beetroot juice).

"Don't worry he's already eaten today, but he did ask us if we would like to join him for a meal tomorrow."

"Quick fly," said Roly Poly.

"Fly," said Dominic.

"Fly," said Bella.

And they started pulling out the heavy wool and dropping it to the ground.

"Quick fly."

Now Ivy, Poppy, Cora and Piper were laughing.

"That's a collie dog with beetroot on his mouth. There's no such thing as hunting sheep."

"We knew that," said Roly Poly, Dominic and Bella, and they started picking up the wool.

That evening Elzamere was pleased. "We met

with Bead and Silk who kindly gave us some homemade clothes, a tub of linen and some other useful things, and you did very well to gather all that wool and find the beetroot. Now I can make some woolly caps and dye them red with beetroot juice."

Later in the evening, the little folk were sitting down on straw cushions. Roly Poly had his feet up on his newly made footrest.

Bella noted, "Oh - it's a footrest not a bookcase?"

Then Dominic asked Edgar, "What happened to Grimweed, Stark and Walter?"

And Edgar told his tale as he knew it, but I will give the full story.

Grimweed, Stark and Walter

One night, when the moon was full, a crowd of little people gathered beneath the sycamore tree. Three goblins, in black cloaks with long pointed hoods full down across their brows, were standing at the back.

Gromley, the elderly gnome, stepped forward to speak. "We have so much to be thankful for with the return of these six young gnomes. We have to praise their courage in their fight against injustice, and especially Edgar, we must thank for bringing light and hope back into their world."

The little people clapped and whistled.

"Three cheers for the six," cried Ted.

"Hip, Hip Hurray!" cheered the crowd. "Hip, Hip Hurray! Hip, Hip Hurray!"

The gnomes beamed, and three goblins at the back moved into a darker space.

The gnomes returned to the farm, and the next day Gromley asked the six young gnomes. "What do you plan doing now?"

Duncan smiled broadly, "I will return to my bakery in the village of Peddlecreek."

"Rosy and I must find another home," Brook said.

"A big one," Rosy added, "now that we have four children. What's life like in Peddlecreek?"

"Wonderful. There's my bakery - and the big folk cottages are not too near and not too far. We have a stream for fishing, fields, woods, and farms. All you need. Yes, it is great. Come to Peddlecreek and we will build you a new home."

He turned to the other gnomes. "All of you - come and visit and stay as long as you like and then we can all help in the building of their home."

"It sounds very nice. We must come and visit," said Robin, and they all agreed.

"We'll meet at Peddlecreek," said the gnomes, "very soon."

Close by, behind the shed, three goblins were waiting, listening and now, like shapeless shadows on a wall, they slipped away.

Duncan returned to his bakery in the village of Peddlecreek. A few weeks later Brook and Rosy arrived with their little ones.

Duncan opened his door. "Come in all of you," he beamed. "You've had a long journey. I have prepared a meal, and made up beds for you tonight."

The four children gnomes were very sleepy. Rosy was holding Rosebud and Junior by the hand, whilst Brook had Bart around his shoulders and Benny in his arms.

"You are very kind," said Rosy.

The baker smiled, "And tomorrow, I will take you to your summer hut. Edgar, Jasper, Guffrey and Robin will be here any day and with all our skills together, you will soon have a permanent home."

The next day they set off early, following a path down towards the fields.

"This way," said Duncan turning. "Follow me," and he slipped beneath the hedgerow into a field of wheat. The family followed close behind. "In the middle of this field you'll see the summer huts."

They walked between golden stalks and sure enough soon came upon, what looked like, a tiny settlement of huts. All the dwellings were round and tapered upwards to a point. Each had windows and single door, and woven neatly in the straw walls were fanciful designs of loops and plaits and little faces.

"They are beautiful and fun!" Rosy exclaimed.

"This is just a summer home." Duncan explained. "When the time comes, the wheat will be cut down. We get plenty of warning, don't worry, and by then your new home will be built."

"And who built this little village, and why for so short a time?" asked Brook.

"The cropper gnomes made these huts," Duncan

explained. "They take great pleasure in their skills and every hut is different. They stay a while, and then move on to make new huts, ever more beautiful."

"Don't they mind? Don't they feel some grief when their homes are destroyed?" asked Rosy.

"No. They don't look back. For the most part they live a simple life and are very peaceful gnomes."

"When will we know the harvest time?" asked Rosy.

"The starlings will make signs in the sky."

Brook and Rosy thanked Duncan. Now the children were running round. "Can we explore?" asked Benny. "Not yet," said Rosy. "Stay close."

"This is your hut," Duncan continued, and he showed the way into a cosy, one roomed dwelling. Inside there were several curved beds to fit the curved inner wall. In the centre was a simple hearth with a grate, a cooking pot and a water pot. On one side stood a long, low table set with straw plates piled high with mushroom pies and twists of bread, and beside these, was a vase of daisies and a note that read: "Welcome Friends."

Rosy hugged her children joyfully. "This is so perfect."

Brook shook Duncan's hand and thanked him once again. "You are a very generous man."

Within a day or so, the other gnomes arrived. Once again Duncan made them welcome and brought them to the huts.

"We have plenty of room here," said Guffrey. "But perhaps we should move in together, for company."

And so they did, but it did not work. Edgar snored, Jasper sang loudly at any time of the day, Guffrey had smelly socks and Robin copied Jasper, but sang out of tune and after just one day they thought it best for each to have their own hut.

The gnomes helped Rosy and Brook with the children and went exploring in the field.

"It's a bit like moving under water," said Brook as he watched the wheat flow in the breeze above their heads.

"Not like the water that I was dragged beneath," said Edgar.

"Tell us again Uncle Edgar," begged the little

ones.

"I was hanging to a branch by my finger nails, my toe nails, the water was thundering in my ears...."

"Look Daddy," Bart pointed upwards. A field mouse was standing between two stems of wheat, gripping either side with his little feet; his tail was wound around a lower stem. He had big ears and big brown eyes, and was gazing down on them. Suddenly the field mouse froze, and then he scurried off.

The next day Duncan took all the gnomes, including the children back to the gnome village where he and his brother cooks ran the bakery. The village was built vertically into the hillside with small shops and dwellings, each with overhanging clumps of soil and grasses like pull-down shutters.

The new home was to be built slightly higher up the hill, and very soon all the gnomes, except for Rosy and the children, began to dig. Rosy and the children went shopping.

They returned late to the summer huts. It was too late to notice that anything was wrong.

Next morning the lads rose early and set off towards the village. Rosy stayed behind with the children.

"I think this place needs a good tidy up," she frowned, "In fact it's quite a mess - like someone's been going through our things."

Suddenly three goblins all cloaked in black were standing at the door.

Grimweed spoke. "We have come for what is ours," he said. "Where is the gold dust? We can make this hard for you or we can make it easy."

"I don't know!" cried Rosy; her eyes were searching desperately for the children.

Walter snatched up Bart. Bart struggled in his arms. Then bit him, jumped down and ran out of the hut. Walter tried again and grabbed Rosebud, while Stark grabbed Brook Junior and held him tight.

"Please don't touch my children. I don't know where it is. I don't know, I don't know," she cried and the children too were sobbing.

"She is telling the truth," said Stark.

"We will be back," he said, "but beware your children may not."

Rosy picked up the cooking pot and flung it at Grimweed. It skimmed passed his head and rolled along the floor. Then she stamped hard on Walter's foot 'Ahhh!' he cried, and she tried to take her daughter back, but the goblin held tight with his bony fingers and pushed Rosy to the floor. Rosebud was still struggling in his arms as he staggered out the hut.

"We want that gold." Grimweed turned, kicked the cooking pot across the room and left.

Stark, with Junior firmly in his grip, followed out.

Rosy was shaking. She ran outside. "Bart!" she called. "Come back!" No sight of him, no sound. "Bart, come back. Rosebud, Junior where are you? Please bring my children back."

As fast as she was able, with Benny in her arms, she ran towards the village, and the village heard her coming.

"My children, they have stolen my children." She was shaking and her heart was thumping. She called again. "They have stolen my children."

All the villagers were soon crowded round. Brook raced over and held his wife as she told him of the kidnap. "The goblins threatened us - if we don't give them gold, they will not return the children. Where is the gold dust?"

"It's at the bottom of the duck pond on the farm."

Right away Guffrey and Robin agreed to fetch the gold dust.

Brook, Rosy, and other gnomes rushed back towards the summer huts. The other villagers soon followed, and a search began.

It was Brook who noticed the line of broken stalks. "This way - we have a clue."

The track led toward a stream. The search party split up. Some gnomes crossed the stream; others went south and followed down to where the stream met the river in the valley. Yet others reasoned, the goblins might travel north towards the distant hills. This group, led by Edgar, took a narrow path beside the stream. They followed on for several hours until they came upon a rocky hill that seemed to rise straight up before them. Here the stream widened to a pool and a small waterfall cascaded from the hills. The gnomes searched the ground for footprints and other signs.

"No footprints, no signs, and no caves." Edgar

was disappointed.

The search continued through most of the night. At last, Edgar said, "We should go back. The others might have news."

But on returning to the huts, they heard the same dismal story - "No sign of goblins." And where was Bart? Poor little Bart had run away, but now, in the night, he came home, and walking just beside him was a field mouse. He ran quickly to his mother and father. They scooped him up and hugged him.

"I fell into a hole and the wind blew and covered me with leaves. I fell asleep for ever so long. Then Duggy came and uncovered me."

"Duggy?" asked Rosy.

"The mouse," he said. "He stayed with me and made me feel safe, and followed me about and when I saw the moon we walked towards it. I heard you talking and here we are. Can we keep him? He's my pet now."

Rosy and Brook wrapped him in their arms.

"If you wanted an elephant today we'd say yes."

"What's an elephant?"

Brook carried his son indoors and sure enough, the

mouse followed. Bart went to bed and his pet settled on the quilt.

Next day the gnomes continued in their search but once again without success. Then returning late that night they found a note pinned to the hut wall.

Brook read the note, "'Leave the gold near the pool at dawn tomorrow. Two gnomes only. They must come alone.'"

Brook clenched his fist. He growled, "I'll go! Let me get my hands on them. I'll pummel them to death."

"Perhaps," said Edgar, "you and Duncan should stay behind with Rosy, Benny and Bart. Jasper and I can meet the goblins and let them know the gold is on its way."

Meanwhile, Guffrey and Robin had made good progress, and after taking lifts on the back of a tractor and a truck they arrived at the farm in just one day.

Gromley and Ted received the news and were horror stuck. They insisted on travelling to Peddlecreek themselves.

"No," said Guffrey, "all that can be done is being done and the whole village of little folk are helping in the search. The goblins said if we give the gold to them they will return the children to us."

Guffrey and Robin went over to the duck pond, removed their dry clothes and dived into the cold, dark water. They dragged the heavy sacks from the water and loaded them onto an old wheelbarrow. The two young gnomes, shivering and muddy, dried themselves beside the fire and dressed. After a quick mug of ale and a meal of grain pudding, they thanked Gromley and Ted and were set to leave at once.

"We have placed food for you onto the barrow and covered everything in leaves. We wish you speed and luck, and hope to hear from you with good news soon."

Guffrey and Robin thanked Gromley and Ted, and waved goodbye, and now pushing the old wheelbarrow, set off through the backfields down towards the lanes.

Edgar and Jasper rose very early and reached the pool by dawn. There was no sign of goblins. The gnomes waited. The sun was rising and the air was cold. The waterfall glistened green against the slimy rocks, and broke across the pool. A single swan glided slowly through the water. Still the gnomes waited. The sun rose higher in the sky. At last, three goblins emerged from the trees. Cloaked and hooded, only their small mean eyes were visible.

"Give us the gold. It's ours." The voice was hard and cruel.

"Ah Stark," said Jasper. He recognised the coarseness of the voice, "You mealy, bug infested rat," and more choice phrases passed his lips.

"You are in no position to insult me. You'll never find the children, never, unless we say, and we won't say not until you return the gold to us."

"It's on the way," said Edgar. "Of course we care more about the children than the gold. It will be here in three days. Be sure of that. It's on the way."

"Very well," said Stark, "you have three days."

The Goblins turned away, their cloaks flapped against the wind, and Edgar and Jasper set off towards the fields.

Now unbeknown to anyone the fairy Jasmine had been watching from the reeds. She had seen Edgar and Jasper arrive and then the goblins. She had seen them talk and turn away. But as the goblins climbed the hill, she let them disappear from sight, for now she had seen something else. A sharp gust of wind had blown the little waterfall aside like a curtain and for just a moment she had glimpsed a cave beyond.

Jasmine flew up and slipped in behind the waterfall. Some light passed through the curtain of water, but still the cave was dark.

"Brook Junior, Rosebud," she called, and then she heard their little cries.

The children were sitting in a large basket. The basket lid was shut and tied with knotted string. The children's eyes were large with fear, and they were sucking on their fingers. There was water in a bowl and some untouched oat biscuits by their side.

The children saw the fairy, "Jasmine, Jasmine. I want my Mummy," and they sobbed.

"I'll soon get you out of here," and she set to undoing the knots. She was skilful, but still it took some time; pulling, chewing, tweaking, threading the string in and out, but at last the string was loose, and she opened up the lid. The little ones climbed out.

"Quick, follow me." Jasmine took them back

further through the cave to where they could hide behind a boulder.

"Let me take your hats," she said and Brook Junior pulled off his blue gnome hat and Rosebud too removed her pink gnome hat and they gave them to the fairy.

"Wait here. I will be back soon. I must prepare for your escape. Don't say a word, not a whisper."

She flew back to the basket, dragged the blanket out and set it on the ground as near as she could to the inner wall of the waterfall. Then she left the cave, flew towards the poolside and hid amongst rushes.

The goblins reappeared. Cautiously and glancing all about they climbed the hillside and entered the cave behind the waterfall.

"What's this?" said Grimweed, staring at the blanket on the ground.

"They've escaped."

"Yes, the basket's empty," Stark rasped.

They raced towards the waterfall, poked their heads through the shower of water and stared downwards at the pool beneath. Two hats, one pink, one blue were swirling in the water.

"They have fallen down and drowned."

The three goblins were angry - as if they had been cheated.

"Oh no! Now we have no children to exchange for the gold."

"We must make new plans." Stark drew the others round and the three wet heads bent together.

"We can't wait until they bring the gold to the pool. We must steal it as soon as it arrives ……"

"We must watch and listen, and take our opportunity…"

"There are more of them than us, but if they don't expect us….."

Each took a dagger and left the cave. They scurried off down the cliff; crossed over to the shadowed waters' edge and disappeared.

The single swan now held the fairy Jasmine waiting in her wings.

When all seemed safe, Jasmine flew back to the cave. She found the children still huddled behind the boulder.

"Hold hands and follow me." She led them forward to waterfall. "Very carefully we will move sideways along this ledge. I'll show you."

Now the wind was very calm and the water fell straight and clear as glass. They shuffled their feet back and forth until they passed behind the waterfall and out. Then slow and carefully Jasmine and the children climbed down the hillside.

"This way." She took them to the swan that was waiting at the waters' edge. Junior and Rosebud stepped gently into the white cradle of the swan's wings. She wobbled just a bit as they settled down.

"Now keep well hidden. No standing up." The children nodded.

The swan raised her yellow beak, quivered her tail briskly and set off. The two children were safe and sound. They felt the gentle rocking movements of the swan and heard the sound of soft swishing as she paddled through the water.

Jasmine had said they must stay sitting down and out of sight, but they peeped through the feathers of the wings to watch the grassy banks that were thick with white and purple flowers and tangled weeds that dipped towards the water. They watched ducks sleeping on the banks and a water vole who plopped himself into the stream and disappeared.

The swan stopped beneath a willow tree. She dipped her head below water surface, and then in a moment reappeared with weeds hanging from her beak. She quivered her tail once more and set off again.

"We're going home, we're going home," sang the little ones.

Ahead of them Jasmine flew swiftly towards the huts. She was through the open door in a flash and landed on Rosy's table. Then taking up a wooden spoon she rattled it against the water pot.

"Rosy," she called and Rosy heard in fact, everybody heard. "Quick, come to the stream, everyone. Your little ones are safe. They are sitting in the cradle of a swan's wings. They will soon be here."

Everybody raced down to the stream. The swan was just coming into view. She proudly wagged her white tail feathers and the children stood up and waved. Everybody cheered and ran towards them. Rosy and Brook swept up their children with hugs and kisses and tears of joy.

Once again, the gnomes had so much to thank a fairy for, and a swan and, it must be said, a gust of wind that revealed to Jasmine the cave behind the waterfall.

The gnomes returned to the huts. All four children were safe and sound.

"We must celebrate," said one village gnome.

"No, no," said Rosy, "It's still not safe. We don't know where the goblins are."

"Duggy, what's the matter?" Bart was watching as his pet chased round and round the hut. Every now and then, the mouse stopped and gazed up at him.

"He's playing," said his mother.

"No, he's not. Duggy doesn't play like that."

Suddenly a dark shadow fell across the field, not from a cloud of rain but a cloud of starlings in the sky. A sign, the sign. Rosy remembered at the time of harvest there would be signs.

"Yes," said Duncan, "It is a sign. We must leave today. The harvest will be tomorrow. We must return to the bakery at Peddlecreek."

Brook turned to Duncan, "What about Robin and

Guffrey?"

"I will go to meet them on the road and tell them what is happening."

The gnomes packed their bags. The furniture was stored beneath hedgerow, and everyone returned to Peddlecreek.

That night the goblins crept along the lines of wheat. They saw the huts, but held back.

"We dare not show ourselves," said Grimweed. "We must watch the huts to see the comings and goings, and watch out for when the gold dust comes."

They stayed awake all night, daring not to sleep, but early in the morning, before the sun was up, the goblins fell asleep.

And early in the morning, before the sun was up, the big folk's combine harvester was rolling through the field.

Just one fairy saw it all and reported back that now, there was nothing more to fear. And indeed nothing more was heard of the goblins Grimweed, Stark or Walter.

Edgar finished his tale. Roly Poly put it bluntly,

"Errh!"

Next day life went on as usual. Dominic, Roly Poly and Edgar went out foraging for food, and the other fairies helped Elzamere to treat the wool. They took the wool, squeezed it, squashed it, washed it to make it soft and clean, and then left it on the roof to dry.

"Wonderful!" exclaimed Elzamere. Then she filled the tub with water, added the beetroot, some other leaves and roots and stirred it with a rusty nail.

"We will leave this to soak for a while, and then add the wool, and you can help me once again. The wool will need to be dried, then teased into tiny strands and rolled around some twigs."

She clapped her pink beetroot coloured hands together. "We will all have red hats. We will all look the same. Like a single troop of little folk."

Cora spoke up. "But we might be mistaken for red berries and be eaten by the birds. No, I don't want to look the same as everybody else. We are all different. I would rather make a hat out of flower petals and seeds. I like being different."

Bella agreed, so did Poppy and Estine. In fact, they all agreed. They all wanted to be different. Elzamere understood - now this was the new easy going Elzamere.

"Yes, on another day we can gather marigolds and gorse to make yellow, lavender to make blue and other flowers and roots to make different shades of red, blue, green and brown. If you want to be different that's fine," she said. Then she put her head on one side.

"Tonight I will tell you a story about someone who was different, but wanted to be the same as everybody else. It might seem like a tall story, but it was a true. It was my uncle Bob who told me and he would never lie."

"Is this a fairy story, or a big folk story?" asked little Ivy.

"Both, but it starts with big folk," said Elzamere.

That evening the little folk settled down and Elzamere began.

A Tale of Hope

"A baby was found at the foot of a tree. She was lying amongst scented leaves, feathers, petals in a basket made of twigs, much like a large bird's nest and she was mewing like a kitten. An old couple out walking their dog saw the basket and heard the tiny cries. They couple peered inside the basket. 'Poor wee dear,' they said.

No one could trace her real parents, so the authorities placed her in a Children's Home. One day, when she was still very small, she was adopted. Now she had parents, brothers, and a home - and a new name - Florence, Flo for short.

Flo was a strange child, very white, as white as a sheet, as white as snow, as white as a ghost, and as she grew older it was clear that people thought her strange.

'Are you ill?' they asked.

It was almost as if the parents were at fault. 'Did they feed her?' Social workers would appear and ask her parents, 'Is she eating enough meat?'

People saw her very white face like some kind of

criticism, like a constant frown, or an exclamation mark. Her school teachers gave her extra milk in the hope she would conform, and some of the children would say, 'You are different. You're not like us.'

Flo was about eight years old, when she first felt a knobbly thing on her back. It itched and she tried to scratch it. Then it erupted and out popped a pair of tiny wings and suddenly she was buzzing like a fly. She had wings. They were only very small, pale, transparent and no use at all. I mean she could not fly.

'Mum what's this - this on my back?' Her mother put on her spectacles and squinted.

'A fly is stuck on your back.' She took a newspaper to swipe at it. 'Oww,' said Flo, 'you're hurting me.' Her mother swiped it once again, and then she flicked it with her finger.

'You are hurting me!' cried Flo and at last her mother realised the wings were firmly attached to her daughter's back.

Her brothers heard and were laughing, and that's when they started calling her Fly. The nickname stuck. 'Here comes Fly,' everyone said, and now she was Fly not Flo.

Her mother took her to the doctor.

'Well,' he said after studying her wings. 'It doesn't run in the family you say?'

'She was adopted.'

'I could refer her to a specialist. I know that some people are born with extra toes, some with webbed feet, some with scaly skin and some might even have a small tail, but I have never heard of anyone who was born with wings.'

He put one hand beneath his chin, fiddled with his stethoscope, and after a moment said, 'There's always the option of amputation.'

'What do you think Flo?' Flo's wings began to buzz. 'Would you like that thing removed?'

'No,' she said firmly, and that was that.

She had to be careful, she did not wish to be the butt of any joke, so to hide her wings she wore extra high swimsuits; always stood with her back to the wall when she changed for gym, and tried very hard not to buzz in public. Her family kept the secret too.

It is possible they forgot, but still they called her Fly, which is quite an ugly name if you think about it.

Flo had two friends who were sisters. One day they said. 'Join us we are in the brownies now,' and Flo joined the brownies. Then they said, 'We are going away with the brownies to the countryside. Come with us,' and she said she would.

At the last minute, the sisters dropped out. 'Our parents have planned another trip.'

'But I only know you two.'

'You'll be OK,' they reassured her.

At this time, Flo's mother was suffering from a sadness disease, which is very common amongst the big folk, and was taken into hospital. The father took control of all domestic matters, and now he began reading the list of things required for his daughter's trip.

'Item 1. Nightie or Pyjamas.'

Flo had never had new pyjamas. In those days, people were quite poor. She was the youngest in the family and had always been given her brothers' hand-me-down pyjamas. They were stripy things with a white cord and a gappy front that served no purpose.

Now her father, he was colour blind. He could see blue and yellow and shades of green, but nothing red, nothing purple, nothing pink, and when he handed his daughter her new pyjamas, he had no idea of their colour.

'Here you are pet,' he said. They were neatly folded, wrapped in cellophane, and they were pink, not just any pink, but PINK like red pink, like the most embarrassed pink.

On the first evening in the camp Flo was careful to hide her wings as she changed into her pyjamas. Then she heard them laughing. Were they laughing at her wings? No the wings were well hidden.

'Look at her pink posh pyjamas.' They laughed aloud and pointed. The comments went on and on. 'Look at her - is she a marshmallow?'

Where were her friends now when she needed them?

Next day the children set out to explore the woods. They came across an opening where the ground sloped down and dipped away. It had been raining hard and all was shiny mud, wet and slimy.

'Hey Fly, can you fly?' said one girl and she grabbed Flo by the arms and pushed her down the slope. Flo slid and slipped and fell hopelessly face down. She was covered head to toe in wet, gooey, muddy clay.

Later sitting in a tin bath (with her back to the wall) no one asked why this girl had a tear running down her cheek.

They all returned home and life went on. But for Flo things were different. Somehow, she had forgotten how to smile.

'Why am I different? I want to be like other girls.'

Now she was sitting in the garden, though, indeed, it was no garden, just scrubby grass and red ants and the only flowers were on the neighbour's lilac tree that hung heavily on the fence - and one small flowering bush.

'One small bush? That's strange,' she thought. 'I've never seen that before. She stared into its plush, pink blooms. And that's when she met my uncle Bob. He was sitting on a petal.

'Hey,' he said, 'we are distantly related.'

She stared. Here before her was a little man with brown and orange wings.

'Do you like my clothes?' he asked. He was wearing a brown velvet waistcoat, short trousers, dark green tights and a pale green shirt.

She could not speak. He let the question pass.

'Yes I believe we are related,' he said.

'Nice to meet you,' she said at last. 'I'm Fly.'

'And I am Bob,' he said, 'Uncle Bob.'

'How can we be related? I'm big, you're small, and excuse me I think you are a fairy.'

'Fairies are not always small, but we always have our magic.'

'But.... ' she began,

'Please call me Uncle Bob.'

'But Uncle Bob, I have wings, yes, but they are ugly like a fly's wings, and I can't fly and I have no magic. I'm not a fairy. I'm just different.'

'Different can be good, and who says you have no magic? What do you think of this peony?'

'It's the most beautiful flower I've ever seen,' she said.

'And what did you think of your new pyjamas?'

'They are a horrible red-pink, the ugliest colour I have ever seen.' Then she realised they were the same colour as the peony. And as true as Bob's my uncle, she smiled.

'That's funny…. They are the same colour.'

'And when you look at that cloud above what do you see?'

She looked up, 'I see a tight, clenched fist. No, that's not it. I see a dove. It all depends how you look at it.'

'And when you hear the name Fly what do you see? What does anyone see?'

'An ugly fly that hangs around bins.'

'But 'to fly' can mean the same as 'hope' and as your uncle Bob I now give to you, your new name - Hope, and this will help you choose how you wish to see things. Hope is the missing link - and so are you.'

And after that she would answer to no other name but Hope."

Now Elzamere had finished the story and Estine asked. "Do you still see your uncle Bob?"

"Sometimes, but mostly he goes his own way."

"And what about Hope?" asked Ivy.

"She's still going strong."

The fairies were very tired having spent the morning jumping up and down on wool.

"Thanks for the story Elzamere," they said as they headed off to bed.

Edgar turned to Elzamere. "Have some more apple juice before you go to bed."

"Thank you, Edgar, I'm grateful."

The old gnome smiled, "and I'm grateful to you Elzamere for all you do for us." They raised their glasses:

"To us, to the fairies and to Uncle Bob."

Major Change

One evening Elzamere was sitting by the window knitting pink and yellow socks for Edgar.

"It's getting darker in the evenings. I'm always busy, busy," she said quietly to herself.

"That is the way of elves," said Edgar, "and some gnomes too."

"And how was life for you Edgar, in Peddlecreek when you were young?"

The fairies heard 'Peddlecreek' and gathered round, hoping for a story. Elzamere placed her knitting down.

"Just as Duncan said, it was wonderful. You know we gnomes learn very quickly."

"Yes, we know that," said Elzamere with a little smile. But in fact, he was not boasting.

"In the gnome world, we can learn a trade, and then if we wish we can learn someone else's trade. I learned carpentry from Robin. From Guffrey I learned to fish. Brook gave me a few secrets of the blacksmith's trade. Rosy taught me the art of pottery and Duncan showed me how to bake a cake, but I must admit I never mastered singing. When Jasper heard me sing, he said something about a broken gate swinging on its hinges.

In truth, we were all Jacks of several trades, and yet we had time to spare for foraging for food and helping Rosy and Brook with their children. We were now their extra uncles, as we gnomes say, and still we had time for playing games. Quick ball, we played in the evenings on the green, (that was a mossy space just beyond the shops) and afterwards we'd go to McTosh's Tavern to drink an acorn cup or two of ale.

One evening Guffrey said. 'Let's celebrate. It's exactly one year since we escaped the caves.'

'Here's to you Edgar.'

'And to you Guffrey,' said I.

'And to you Duncan.'

We all raised our acorn cups.

'To you Jasper,' and soon we had drunk six, seven acorn cups of ale. I lost count.

'And, to the children.' Now we were all beginning to slur our words..

'Let us sling, I mean sing…'

'In the merry month of May,

Maaaawy…The bells were ringing
and we were singing Hay Haaay….
In the merry month of June…We sailed the sky
away in a red balloooon…
All six of us and you came toooo.
We sailed away awaaaay……'

'What comes next?'…..

'In the merry month of July… Let's play darts.'

A dartboard made from twigs and moss was set up in the corner. Now with frowns, squints, and all at once, we threw our grass darts at the board. We all missed.

'Time gentlemen please.'

'Righto McTosh.' We waved our caps and left.

Our rooms were set into the hillside just above the shops. Usually we would leave a ladder out to climb back up.

'Wheth's the ladder?' asked Jasper with a sudden lisp. He went looking for the ladder behind some bins - 'Clatter, bang.' 'I can't find it.'

'S'let's not wake the neighbours,' said Guffrey. He was searching round looking for a foothold in the hillside wall. 'Now, I know…. there's one here somewhere.' He crouched down and that gave me an idea.

'If I stand on your back I'll reach the second foot hole,' and I did.

'Oy!' said Guffrey. 'Don't stand on a fisherman's back. You come down. I will stand on your shoulders.'

'And I'll stand on your shoulders,' said Robin.

'And I on yours,' said Duncan to Robin.

'Duncan your bakery issover tharr - ground level,' Robin gestured. Now Duncan raised his hand above his brow as if to seek a far horizon. He staggered off and rattled at his door.

I thought we were making almost no noise, but suddenly heads were popping out of windows.

'There will be consequences,' said a grumpy looking gnome from up above. His greasy hair was sticking out beneath his nightcap. It was Lurgie. He and his father and stepsister were new to the area.

'You'll wake my father and he's very important you know. You can't make all those drunken noises, waking everybody up and not face the consequences.'

'Can we borrow a ladder?'

Next day we all had headaches. At least I did when I rolled out of bed. 'Uh.' I said. I saw my red-eyed reflection staring back at me from the mirror.

'Should be ashamed of yourself,' it said. I must admit I was in a shabby state and the inside of my mouth felt like I had eaten a thistle with a slug on it.

I washed and dressed. I thought 'I'll have a dip in the stream. That will bring me round.'

Anyway, I was soon walking along the path, minding my own business, when who do you suppose I met? - Lurgie with his father and his stepsister.

'Father - he's one of them,' said Lurgie, pointing a bony finger in my direction. I turned to look behind me. 'Who was he talking about?'

The father, a big gnome with beady eyes and starchy looking whiskers, frowned and said, 'I see,' and then to me he said, 'I am Major Basset.'

'Nice to meet you... - Mr Basset. I'm Edgar.' But I was looking at his daughter as if we'd just been introduced. She was very pretty, with wide hazel eyes, glossy pink curls and freckles and she smiled at me, an impish smile. The major looked at his daughter then at me and scowled.

'Major Basset!' he said, stressing the 'Major'.

'Yes sir, eh Major Basset.'

'Late last night you and your friends were making a commotion, disturbing the peace. I received complaints.'

'Sorry, but we were celebrating. It was an anniversary.'

'Take this as a warning. Any other loutish behaviour from you or your friends and I will take the matter further, and there will be consequences.'

Lurgie was looking at me and smirking, as if to say 'I told you so.'

I walked away in a dream. I forgot the morning dip and went over to the bakery. They were all sitting in the kitchen, all except Jasper. He was having a long lie in. I related the meeting to the others. My most important question was 'What's her name?'

Rosy answered. 'That's Meadowsweet. She's the stepdaughter of Major Basset.'

'Meadowsweet.' I said 'a name sweet like honey wine.'

'How's your head?' asked Duncan. 'I think we all had a bit too much to drink. Here help yourself to a strong cup of acorn tea, and then help me bring a sack of flour from the front.'

I drank the tea and made my way towards the shop front, and there before me, standing at the counter, was Meadowsweet.

'Hello Meadowsweet.'

'Hi,' she said, 'you're Edgar.'

'Yes,' I beamed.

'And I am Guffrey,' said Guffrey appearing out of nowhere.

'And I am Robin.' She smiled at Robin and Robin blushed. Where did they all come from?

'And I am Duncan, the baker.'

'Of course I know you are the baker.' She smiled (that impish smile).

'And how can I help you? How about some honeydew crumble, freshly baked?'

'Yes, and some corn pudding and a loaf please.'

'Right pass your basket over,' said Duncan.

We were standing around looking rather foolish, at least the others were.

'The sack is outside, just over there,' said Duncan nodding at the door. 'Thanks.'

As Meadowsweet was leaving Guffrey asked, 'Do you like fish?'

I did not think much of his chat up line, but it seemed to work.

'Yes, I love fish.'

'If you don't know this area, there's a beautiful stream with whopping great stickle backs. I can show you how I fish and you can have fish tonight for supper.'

'Yes,' she smiled.

'We could all do with fish tonight,' said I and Robin agreed.

'And we'll come too,' Rosy was standing at the kitchen door. 'I will bring the children. Duncan will you join us?'

We met at 3 O'clock.

There was Guffrey, 'We take this flea and attach it to this hook here. You should come and see my fishing boat. It's moored further up the stream towards the river.'

'What - you mean that old shoe canoe?' Duncan quipped. 'It lets in water.'

'It does not. I sealed it myself and it is far from being a shoe canoe, it's the best.'

'Yes the best,' we joked.

'….stand back little ones as I cast the line.'

Now everyone was sitting quietly on the bank. I said, 'Hey children let's play throw the roll.' Soon the little ones were squealing, running up and down and throwing tangled straw for Duggy.

'You will frighten the fish,' said Guffrey sternly.

'Okay,' I said 'We'll move over there. Meadowsweet will you play throw the roll and help me with the children.'

'In just a moment,' Meadowsweet replied. And when Guffrey had settled down with his fishing rod, she smiled, tapped him on the arm and left him to his fish.

And so it was that Guffrey and I were to be rivals for the love of Meadowsweet. Still we did all things together as friends: walks beside the stream and up towards the waterfall; foraging for food; picnics in the meadows. I remember it seemed like one long summer. But, was it me or Guffrey that she loved?

We had not seen Major Basset for several weeks. He and Lurgie were away on business. Then one day he returned. He was standing on the path just outside the bakers. He cleared his throat.

'There will be a meeting tonight on the green.' He said and he spoke so loudly, it seemed as if at any moment he would say 'March' and we would all march.

'Everybody needs to be there. The meeting will be held at 8 O'clock. Please inform all villagers who are not here now they must attend.'

We were there at 8.00, all of us. In any case, I had wanted to see Meadowsweet. She was there standing beside her father and Lurgie, looking a little downcast I recall. I smiled but she did not see me.

'I have the sad news that our dear friend Gromley has passed away. One day he was there, the next day he was gone. I do not believe he suffered. There will be a memorial for him in a week's time in his Uplands Village, and I am informed, anyone who wishes, may attend.'

There was a murmur of shock. We were all shocked. Such a lovely man, and poor Ted.

'I must also inform you that as he was the Head of the Council of Little Folk this responsibility now lies with me. I am to take his duties upon my shoulders.'

'That's a bit quick,' we thought, but we were still too shocked to take that in.

The memorial was held at midnight in the backfield of the farm. It was a cold night. The sky was bright with stars. We lit our little candles and sang songs of love and respect for Gromley. Then Jasmine, her voice pure and clear, sang a farewell song. As she finished, we blew our candles out, gazed upwards to the sky and said farewell.

We returned to Peddlecreek, but it seemed things would never be the same. For one thing, there were rules - rules written out and stuck here, there and everywhere - on walls, on bins, on windows:

'No parking wheelbarrows here.'

'No sacks to be left outside the shop fronts.'

'No quick ball on the green.'

'No washing to be seen hanging from the windows.'

'No ladders after 10.00pm.'

'No drinking after 9.00pm.'

'All field mice and other pets to be kept on leads'

Lurgie would appear strutting up and down the path wearing a tall black hat and carrying a polished walking cane. He would go 'tap flick, tap flick' with his stick. You could hear him coming. Then he'd stop, and in the silence you would hold your breath as he placed his nose against a window, then turning once more, he would walk on - 'tap flick, tap flick,' and you could draw breath again.

One day he surprised us all. He was walking slowly along the path pushing a bicycle. The bike was squeaking. For each revolution of the wheels, there were two squeaks and a clunk.

A child was watching from the side, 'It squeaks,' the child pointed out. Lurgie stopped. From his pocket, he pulled out an oily rag, flicked it in the air and then screwed it in a ball.

'I'm still working on it.'

We had never seen a gnome with a bicycle. What would be the point? We have no real roads and on the big folk roads, gnomes would have no more chance than hedgehogs in the traffic.

'What's that for?' The child pointed to a trailer box at the back.

'Luggage or a passenger may be,' Lurgie informed the onlookers. Then he placed his right foot upon the pedal, leaned forward, pushed off and in a smooth proficient movement raised his left leg up and over. His left foot found the left pedal and he cycled off. It was very impressive except for the squeak squeak clunk, squeak squeak clunk'.

We saw less and less of Meadowsweet, and when we did, she looked sad. Her eyes seemed to have grown half the size again, and her eyebrows were almost meeting in the middle.

One day I met Meadowsweet as she came into the bakery.

'Please Meadowsweet I need to talk to you. When can we meet?' - squeak squeak clunk, squeak squeak clunk.

'Shush.' Lurgie passed us by.

'It's difficult, but meet me at the first corner of the cornfield at 9.00 tonight,' and as she turned to leave she said, 'Yes and bring the others too.'

Just when I wanted to proclaim my love, I had to tell the others, 'You come too.'

'This is very serious,' said Meadowsweet. It was 9.00 on the dot and we were standing in a group at a corner of the field. 'He, that is my stepfather, plans to change everything, to control you all like…..' and she trailed off. 'Soon I'll be sent away. I have no sympathy for his aims, but worse as far as he is concerned, because he is superstitious, he fears that a female relative living under the same roof will spoil his campaign plans.

'Where will you go?' She looked very sad. I wanted to take her in my arms and say. 'No one will control you and no one will control us. We are free gnomes, living in a free world.'

'I will try to keep in touch and send messages to all of you my friends.' And before we knew it she had turned and left. We followed blindly in the darkness, but there was no sign of Meadowsweet. 'Come back,' we called but she did not.

We returned to the village, climbed the ladder to Major Basset's apartment and knocked at his door.

'What do you want?' Major Basset snapped at us.

'We want to see your stepdaughter. We want to know that she is well. She is our friend. We care about her. Is she here?'

'Of course you can see her. Yes, she has been ill. You might not know this, but now she is being sent away to convalesce.'

'Where is she going?'

'Manners please. We have not quite decided. Lurgie bring your sister here.'

Lurgie appeared holding Meadowsweet's arm, rather too tightly for my liking.

'Your friends are here and want to know that you are well, but you are not, are you?' She went to speak, and I swear Lurgie gripped her arm more tightly. 'No,' continued the Major 'and now you have to go away to recover.'

'Yes,' she murmured.

'Now will you excuse us,' and he closed the door.

Again we knocked, and then again. Eventually he opened up.

'Now if you do not go I will call the police and have you arrested.'

This was the first time any of us had heard of police in Peddlecreek. Now Meadowsweet stepped between us with her back to her father and pleaded.

'Please, please go. I'll be OK,' she said. Then she silently mouthed the words. 'I will send a message.'

Later that evening, we heard more bad news. Jasper announced. 'I've been thinking - I want to leave, I want to travel to find myself and find my music.'

We were somehow unsurprised. Of all of us, Jasper craved freedom most.

'I will return - you are my friends.'

That night he left. We stood in a line, Guffrey, Robin, Duncan, Brook and I. We said farewell and waved. Then each one of us watched silently as our skinny friend, waved back to us, turned and disappeared into the tall grasses of the fields.

He was not the only gnome to leave. One day our neighbour Tim Othea said, 'Did you know it will soon be illegal to forage in the woods without a licence? We are getting out while we can.'

The dark days came. Meadowsweet was gone. We waited for her message, but none came.

More talk, more rumours: - 'The Square Heads are coming.' Who were the Square Heads? Then one day a notice board appeared - and notices:-

'Workers are required to build a new prison. Good pay. No experience necessary.'

'Interested in a new career? Join the Police Force. Good pay and holidays.'

No one from Peddlecreek applied to build the prison or to join the Police Force, yet workers came, and near the hilltop, the land was hacked away. And Police - we soon saw police. It was just a small group of gnomes and goblins. They all looked much the same to us, their whiskers waxed and twirled and their uniforms cream and black. They marched in step, stamping up and down the path.

'Well they do look smart,' some were heard to say, while others whispered something else entirely.

One grey day Major Basset called a meeting on the

green.

'We all know the dangers of the Square Heads,' he said, (we knew nothing). 'They are our common enemy, and I can tell you, there will be war. Certain rules must now be set forth. There will be no more meetings to he held beneath the sycamore tree. A special group of my experts will make all decisions and taxes will be charged. I know that you have never paid taxes. It is a big folk thing, but some things that the big folk do are good.'

'What?' asked Duncan.

'Do you mind I'm still speaking - as I say, it will necessary for you to pay taxes so we can fight the Square Heads.'

The rain began to fall. It was slow at first.

'And what do we use to pay these taxes - turnips?' I asked.

'Such matters will be worked out in due course.'

Now the rain was falling hard. Major Basset moved to go. We lads stepped forward. Lightning lit the sky and the distant hills were bright for just a moment.

'Can you tell us, where is Meadowsweet? Is she

well?' Robin asked. Wind and rain crashed, thunder boomed.

The major turned on his heel. 'I have important business,' he said pulling up his collar.

'Where is Meadowsweet? When will she return?' We pressed more questions to him.

'In truth,' he said, 'I have sent her where she is safe. Edgar despite you and your friends' often-loutish behaviour, I hear you are a clever gnome. Hear me then when I say Meadowsweet is safe. After all, I am her father. Now come you lads, join the army. It is your duty anyway to fight the Square Heads. If you join now you will soon be officers, but if you wait until you are conscripted you will be mere privates.'

As dreadful as this all sounded we stood our ground.

'But where is Meadowsweet?' Robin asked again.

'Yes where?' said I.

'She is by the coast. The sea air will do her good,' the major waved his arm, 'I will say no more. Now if you wish to join the army, speak to my son Lurgie over there. He is taking names.'

Later we were sitting in Brook and Rosy's kitchen. Robin asked. 'Have you noticed all the fairies have disappeared?'

'They are in the woods,' said Rosy. She was holding Benny and Bart on her lap, while Brook junior was standing on her chair behind her with two arms looped around her neck. Rosebud was playing with Duggy on the floor.

'We must go and find them. They might know something,' said I. But just then, a small head appeared at the window.

'How did I know you would call me?' It was Jasmine. She flew inside.

'We are so happy to see you,' we said.

Jasmine was breathless. She found a cushion, sat down cross-legged and shook her turquoise wings, 'Sorry, it is wet out there,' she said like someone with a wet umbrella.

'I have no news of Meadowsweet, but I believe she is safe. Tonight I must return to the woods. I can say little at this stage, but I must ask three of you to follow me.' Guffrey, Robin and I agreed to go. Then to the others she said, 'If anyone should ask you where they are, say your friends have gone fishing and will return in a few days time, as they surely will.'

Then Jasmine asked mysteriously. 'Can you bring a ladder and a sack of food?'

We set off into a stormy night of darkness, wind and rain. I took one end of the ladder, Robin took the other and Guffrey walked alongside carrying the sack. We travelled through the woods close behind Jasmine's tiny glinting lights. At first we heard scratching in the undergrowth, but as we moved more deeply into darkness all we heard, above our hastened breaths, was the swish of rain on leaves and the scrunching of our boots upon the sodden earth. On and on we travelled through the night.

At dawn, the rain stopped, the birds began to sing, and the morning light broke through and glistened on the leaves and puddles.

'We are here,' Jasmine announced at last.

And we were, so to speak, for we were face to face with the Square Heads."

Edgar stopped telling his tale. He stretched out his

legs, puffed out his cheeks and rubbed his head. He looked set for bed.

"Oh Edgar, what happened next?" the fairies begged.

"Really I'm stiff."

"Please Edgar what happened next?"

"Okay," he continued.

The Square Heads and Illwilly

"Well two men with square heads and blue faces, came forward. The three of us were shocked. Well I was, I must admit. Then the first square head growled 'RWARW'.

'Is that any way to welcome guests?' asked Jasmine.

'No I was just practising.' Then both the Square Heads removed, what we now saw to be their square blue hats. Their own heads beneath were perfect, normal domes.

'Glad to meet you.' We spoke quickly, and nervously, and putting down our load, we wiped our palms and moved to shake their hands.

'Sorry,' said one as he waved his hand, 'the dye's still wet - it's woad. But welcome Edgar, Guffrey and Robin. You don't recognise us? It is I… your neighbour, Tim Othea and here's my brother Jack. Come join us. Our camp is over here.'

We followed Tim to a clearing where we met a group of, may be thirty, gnomes. They were all busy making things with straw. They looked up and greeted us. We handed over the sack of food and the ladder, and then Tim explained their plan. And this was the plan…"

Edgar turned to the fairies. "But no. First, I must tell you about Illwilly. Amongst the old gnomes he was a myth, or a superstition or a truth, I'm not sure which. Anyway it was said that Illwilly would appear when the little folk grew hateful towards each other, and soon afterwards, a misfortune would befall us all, with a famine, a flood or plague - or perhaps all three.

The plan….yes, I will use Tim's words to explain," said Edgar.

"'It's all lies. A lie for a lie, and truth for truth, say I. There were no Square Heads, only us poor folk. Yes, Basset invented an enemy so that he could rule with fear, and now we will give him back his lies with knobs on. I would like you to meet the cropper gnomes. They know the art of making things from straw.'

The busy gnomes looked up again and smiled. Then Tim showed us a battalion of soldiers - straw soldiers. Newly painted blue, they were hanging out to dry beneath the branches of a tree. We walked over.

'Now each one of us will have to carry three at least,' said Tim. 'They're not heavy, you might manage four. Some don't even have legs. We will put them at the back, and stand them on a stone or something. Then there are the straw swords, the shields, and of course, we do have a few bows and arrows, real ones, I mean. I hear the Major is a superstitious man - that is luck for us, as we have a superstition for him. Here we have the head of Illwilly. Horrible isn't he?'

We had to admit it was the most horrible face we had ever seen. The cropper gnomes were certainly artists with great skills.

'And now we shall have a pair of stilts, made from the ladder, so Illwilly will soon have legs. We have an army, an army of straw may be, but we will beat the Major and send him packing. The fairies will leave today to inform all those who need to know that what is to be revealed tomorrow night, is not to be believed.'

Then Tim asked, 'Are you with us? We fight for freedom and for dignity.'

'Yes,' we said, and if we had our doubts, we did not show them as we joined the chorus, 'For freedom and for dignity.'

It turned out that Guffrey was the best at walking on the stilts, so he was to be Illwilly, and he practised for a while. Then, as we three gnomes had travelled through the night, we rested, and in the early afternoon, we slept. Next day, we were up before the dawn and ready. Robin and I, painted blue with square hats upon our heads, took the straw soldiers and carried them before us. Guffrey too, was loaded down. Beneath one arm, he carried the stilts, and beneath the other, he held the evil looking, ghastly head of Illwilly.

We were there in Peddlecreek by evening - all of us, the rebels, the croppers, and the straw battalion. We held back beyond the fields. Then several lads followed up around the hilltop, just above the prison, and with stealth slipped down behind the prison guards. These inexperienced, unwary guards were quickly overpowered. Now the way was clear and our brave blue soldiers, brought out several rows of straw soldiers, stood them shoulder to shoulder and waited on the hilltop.

The rest of us moved forward from the fields. We lined our soldiers up in full view of Peddlecreek. We all looked mean, grim and formidable and while the sun was yet edging towards the west, we heard a scream. I think it was Rosy screaming, and others were yelling: 'Look the Square Heads are coming!'

The Major and his son clambered down their ladder, astonished, I would say. This was not a war on their terms.

'Police!' the Major called and a few cream and black shirted gnomes and goblins emerged waving battens. They tried to be brave even when they saw the blue faced, square headed enemy beyond, but they were too few before so many and they thought they might fight better from the windows and the hilltop. They turned about and looked up.

'Guards!' called the Major. He too looked up towards the hilltop where the Square Heads were amassed waving swords and knives. They clearly held the hilltop. The Major, not easily defeated, turned once again and looked towards us. Once again, someone screamed, 'Look Illwilly!' I think it was Rosy. Then all the villagers, so it seemed, were crying out: 'Illwilly!'

Indeed Illwilly was striding tall behind our ranks, sneering with his ugly grin, his fork like teeth jutting out, his glassy eyes ablaze with hate, and we plain, square headed, blue faced lot were roaring and waving our weapons. Then in a moment, the sun was gone, darkness fell and all was silent. We waited, and we waited.

Suddenly a familiar sound: - squeak squeak clunk, squeak squeak clunk, squeak squeak clunk, squeak squeak clunk, squeak squeak clunk, quicker and quicker and then more distant until the sounds grew small and disappeared completely."

Edgar stretched his legs. "Now I'm off to bed." He said. "If you want to know what happened next you will have to wait until tomorrow."

On the following evening the fairies were eager to listen to his tale.

Sea Mists and High Hopes

Edgar began, "The fairies had hoped to see the Major driven out, and now they followed behind the cyclist and his passenger as they squeaked and rattled through the night.

Peddlecreek began to return to normal. The police and guards disappeared surprisingly quickly. People began to smile again; to relax; to sing; to let their washing hang to dry; to let their field mice roam; to play quick ball on the green. In many ways life returned to normal. Yet where was Meadowsweet?

Then within a week, the fairy Jasmine returned with news. Once again, we were sitting in the kitchen at the bakery. Jasmine began, 'Meadowsweet is at the Major's ancestral home. The Major's old father, the late Lord Basset had six sons, all born at one time. There was great rivalry amongst the sons. Finally, they all decided to leave and seek their fortunes. The Major became a major, but I don't believe he was ever in a war.'

'You make a great detective Jasmine,' said I. 'We are impressed.'

'Lupine and the other fairies have remained behind and are watching in case the Major and Lurgie take Meadowsweet elsewhere.' She continued. 'The ancestral home is on the coast - a small area in a tiny bay with a sandy beach. On the landside in every direction, there are hills with thick, almost impenetrable woods. We had to follow close behind the Major for fear of losing him. In fact pretty soon the bicycle broke down and was abandoned, so from then on we had no clues from the squeaks as to their whereabouts.'

Guffrey, Robin and I decided, come what may, we would rescue Meadowsweet from her overbearing family, and soon we had plans to do just that. One morning the three of us waved a quick goodbye to our friends and with our wheelbarrow heaped with useful items, we set off down towards the stream, then onwards to the river where Guffrey's dinghy was moored. Yes, the dinghy named Honeybee was small but despite our jokes, not quite the shoe canoe. She had a sail and four rowlocks and oars for rowing. On the deck itself, there were fishing rods, ropes, and bins, some with lids some without, and everything smelled of fish.

Guffrey saw our faces. 'You'll get used to that,' he said with a grin.

The boat was held close to the bank by a rope looped around tree stump. Guffrey untied the rope, and using the oars, we pushed the Honeybee free from the bank. She slid through the water, and with a little tugging and pushing here and there, we were soon out into a stretch of open water. At first, she rocked gently in the swell. Then Guffrey called, 'hold tight' and now we rocked widely in the wake of a big folk boat that passed us by on the other side of the river.

'You'll get used to that as well,' said Guffrey.

Robin and I took the oars while Guffrey sat astern at the rudder, and rowing hard we travelled for some time along the river. Gradually it widened towards the estuary, where other rivers fed the flow, and for some time, we followed with the tide. Then we saw two, may be three huge vessels chugging, churning through the mud-grey water, and still we rowed steadily.

Our tiny vessel held close towards the bank, but then moving over to the other side we rocked and rolled in cross currents that buffeted and sent sprays across our bow. How the Honeybee rose and fell. Then Guffrey, his eyes set against a low horizon, turned and the three of us gnomes, in a fishing dinghy reached the open sea. We put the oars aside and raised the sail. The wind was good and now we raced across the waves. Guffrey called to us to move this way that way, to pull this rope, that rope and we strained to hear him above the sound of waves and wind and sea gulls that suddenly loomed above.

'One of the hazards of the sea,' said Guffrey looking up, and for sure, a seagull is a fearful foe to us small gnomes.

'Take these,' and he handed us each a long handled bat from amongst his fishing tackle.

We did what we could. With one hand, we held the bat and jabbed it at any seagull that swooped too low. With all else we held our balance in a rolling sea.

After a while, the seagulls gave up and soared away towards the shore. We continued on unmolested, travelling North, Northwest following the coastline. After some time Guffrey pointed to a lighthouse further up the coast and called to us, but his words were lost. We sailed on through the bright, sunlit sea with our ruddy faces set towards the sun and gusting winds - we were natural sailors I would say. Then all at once, we saw against the far horizon a clash of pink, orange and purple - a brilliant sunset. The three of us watched in awe until the sun slipped down and disappeared.

Gradually the air grew cool and calm and a full moon showed weakly through a pearl grey mist. Guffrey lowered the sails and once again, we took the oars and rowed towards the coast. We landed on a sandy beach, and out we jumped, the three of us, and dragged the dinghy up across the sands towards the dunes.

Jasmine had suggested we meet here, just before the perils of the rocks. She said she was no sailor and would prefer to fly. There was no sign of Jasmine. No doubt, she would arrive soon enough. You cannot pin a fairy down to time. We took provisions from the dinghy, prepared our evening meal and sat down to eat. Then we slept.

Next morning I was slowly waking, stiff limbed and wondering where I was. Then I felt the spray. The tide was coming in. My woolly socks were getting wet.

'I didn't want to wake you,' said Guffrey.

'Fine,' I said squeezing my socks around my toes, and then I took the cup of nettle tea he offered me.

'Thanks,' I said. 'The mist has not quite cleared. Is there no sign of Jasmine yet?'

'No, but I think we should travel on. She can catch us up.'

'I agree,' said Robin. 'We have no time to lose.' He was set to go.

'Okay,' I said as I was pulling on my boots. Then I shoved a few things into a sack and flung the sack across my back.

'We march - but Robin, it's not like you to be impatient.'

'Perhaps you don't really know me.'

This was unexpected. 'Okay, okay. Let's go.'

The three of us set off, one behind the other with our sacks. We carried enough provisions for a few days. At first, we moved easily across the sand, over salt glazed weeds, around rock pools with their crawling sea tide life, and over pebbled dunes, up towards the black, pitted rocks, where we hoped to find the upper path. We jumped from one rock to another, expertly - that is we did not fall, but hopelessly - for it seemed we made no progress.

'There has to be an easier way,' said I.

'There is.' It was Jasmine standing on a rock just above our heads. She was wet and windblown, her hair a tangled mop, and her wings were now a flaming pink.

'You could have waited for me, and it's your fault I'm late!'

With her hands on hips and toes tapping, I thought, 'That's a very angry fairy.'

'Jasmine - wonderful to see you,' I called.

'Hi there - Jasmine,' said the other two.

'You all forgot the spot pot,' she said. 'Do you realise how heavy it was for me to fly with? And now you are setting off without me.'

'Was she going to cry? No. Was she going to throw the spot pot? Well yes I guessed, quite possibly.'

'Jasmine,' said Guffrey, 'we'll all go down and have a nice cup of nettle tea and a crumble bun. See what I have in my sack?'

'You should have put the spot pot in your sack,' she snapped. 'Okay I'll come down. You are going the wrong way anyway. Never mind nettle tea, I must tell you there were heavy rains round here a few days ago. Taking the high road will prove impossible. We must go by boat. We can follow up around the rocks towards the bay. I'm sure this will prove no problem for us.'

So now we took the Honeybee back down to the sea and climbed aboard. Once again, Robin and I started rowing.

'I'm tired,' said Jasmine yawning slightly. She found a space in the bow and fell asleep.

A mist descended once again.

'Guffrey will we make it round the cliffs?' asked Robin.

'Yes keep up the pace. Hardly any wind, just a little mist. I can still see where the sun is, I know the time of day, and I can feel the tide.'

'Are you sure we can make it?' said I.

'Am I sure? Do you mind? I'm an experienced sailor.'

It seemed like an argument was about to brew. We were all edgy, including me. I thought the mist more like a moving cloudbank. I found the rowing hard and my socks were wet.

Jasmine woke, 'I feel sick. Everything smells of fish,' she complained. Her wings were very green.

Then we heard a foghorn. 'Whose idea was it to come by boat?' 'Hers.' 'His.' 'Yours.'

But suddenly the mists lifted. Sunlight lit the sea. Yes, surely, the mists had lifted, yet strangely, we were still in shade - and gazing up we saw the reason why - we were in the shadow of the lighthouse. It towered above. Then looking down we saw black rocks beneath the chopping waves.

Hard and fast we rowed against the tide until finally the waters changed to green for go.

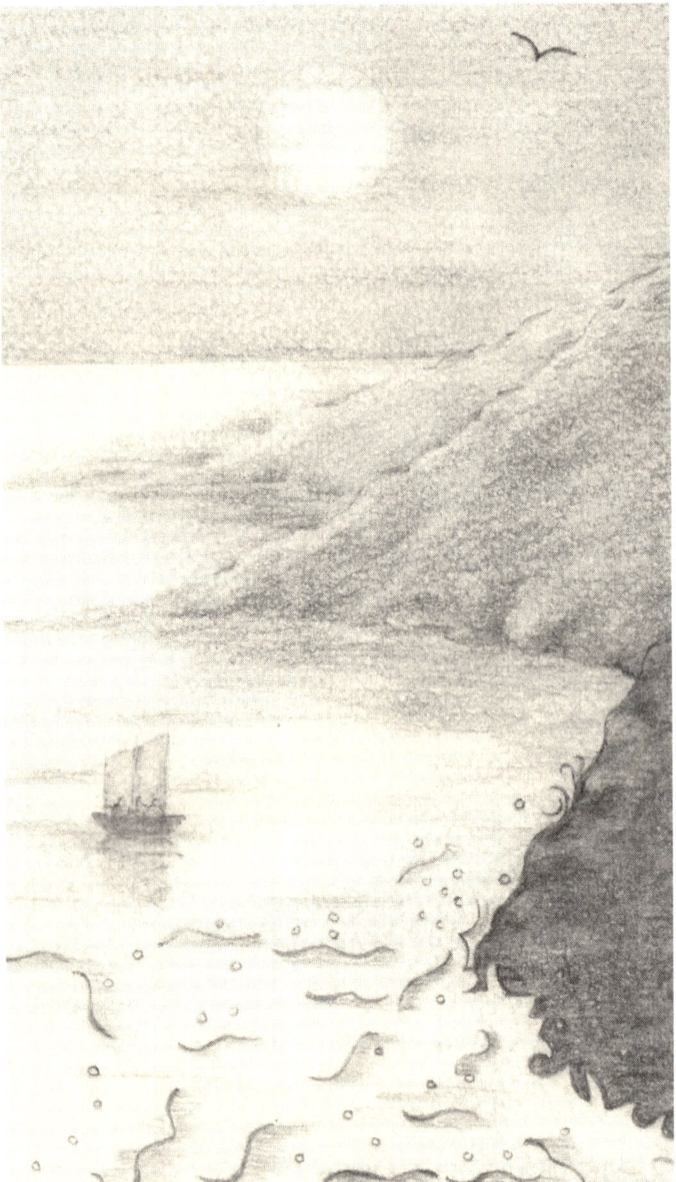

Guffrey raised the sail, and as the wind picked up the Honeybee cut through the waves, and curved smoothly out to sea, then once more, we turned towards the coast and swiftly sailed until we reach the bay beyond.

'We have made it,' said I, as we pulled the dinghy up across the sandy beach.

'Yes,' said Robin.

'Of course,' said Guffrey.

We all stood back, gazing up and studying the cliff above. Where was the Manor Hall? We stared blankly for a while, and then gradually made out the outline of a building. The Manor Hall - more like a rock itself - was disguised. The crevices and crenulations of its walls, turrets and pillars were masked by grass and lichen. A single door, set back, was barely visible. The windows too, and jutting sills like bird perches in the cliff, were stained and edged with moss. The roof was cast in shade by trees that hung entangled from the overreaching heights.

'It's like a long forgotten prison,' I thought. 'Poor Meadowsweet.'

A small treacherous looking path zigzagged up

against the cliff face.

'Yes,' said Jasmine watching our doubtful, upturned faces, 'You can climb that way. I must fly,' she said. 'I have to find Lupine and the others. I will take the spot pot now. See you soon.'

With just a flicker of her now greenish wings, she was off.

We set to climbing up the rock path. One by one, it was a tight fit for us, and we were wary of slipping and falling to our deaths. There was barely a handhold, ridge or bulge to hang on to, but of course, we had experienced worse than this. Eventually the path followed around and led up towards the door. Robin stepped forward and rang the bell. After some moments, the door opened. An elderly, somewhat ailing looking gnome, peered down from inside, which was several steps above us.

'We are old neighbours of the Major and Lurgie and Meadowsweet,' said Robin.

'Neighbours you say and your names are…..'

'I am Robin and this is Guffrey and Edgar. We have important news for the Major. Can we speak with him?'

'What!' said the Major, like a blast from the past. He was standing just behind the elderly gnome.

'And what could you possibly have to say to me - oh very well enter.'

We followed into a dark, wood panelled room overlooking the sea.

'We were passing on a fishing trip.' We did in fact look sea worn, and smelt of salt and fish.

'We have good news - all's clear,' said I.

'Do you mean the Square Heads have gone?'

'No not exactly. They're not so bad. Live and let live I say. No I mean, it's all clear - the plague has gone.'

'What plague?'

'The blue spot plague. It's gone. Have you heard nothing of it?' Robin asked.

The major looked horrified and visibly shrank back from us.

'Thank you for your news, but now I think you should be going.'

'Is there any chance we could speak with Meadowsweet?' asked Robin.

'Yes, is she well?' I asked.

'You can't see her. In fact, she has taken to her bed. No she is not feeling well.'

Then Meadowsweet appeared at the door. She was wearing a blue dressing gown and fluffy slippers and was holding a small pink handkerchief against her nose.

'Oh I could hear your voices. I knew it was you. It's true I'm feeling poorly, but I just had to say hello to my old friends from Peddlecreek.'

'I think you should go back to bed Meadowsweet,' said the Major.

'Yes, but first I would like a cup of water.'

The butler was called and asked to bring some water. He returned quickly carrying a jug and an acorn cup.

'Thank you Pritchley,' she said and removed her handkerchief to drink.

We gasped. Blue spots were breaking out around her chin and nose.

'What's the matter?' she said all opened eyed and innocent.

We tried to appear as helpful as possible. 'It's not that contagious,' we said stepping back.

'It can be curable especially in the young,' Guffrey advised.

'We have heard of several reliable treatments,' added Robin.

The major looked fearful - for his stepdaughter or for himself? - I wondered.

'What treatments, cures?' he asked in a small, croaky voice.

'Seawater, fresh air, and onions,' we informed the Major.

'You seem to know all about it. What should I do?'

'We could try the seawater first. We should all go down to the beach.'

'I think you three should take Meadowsweet. I have something else I have to do.'

'Should I change?' asked Meadowsweet.

'No, no,' said the Major, 'go quickly, go as you are.'

As we left we heard the major call out to Pritchley: 'Onions!'

Robin, Guffrey and I climbed slowly and carefully down the little path, but Meadowsweet was surefooted. She still held her handkerchief up against her nose, but I believe I saw a smile beneath.

When we reached the bottom, we headed for the dinghy and set off. We were soon out to sea.

'What a wonderful cure this is.' Meadowsweet dipped her handkerchief into the seawater and washed away the blue.

We headed south blown by a gentle breeze.

'I will write a letter to father. Jasmine said she would deliver it.'

Meadowsweet wrote:

'Dear father, thank you for all you have done for me. But now I am a big girl and wish to leave home. I hope that one day you will come to visit me in Peddlecreek. May be one day I can visit you, that is, when I am well,

Love from Meadowsweet.'"

"So that was a happy ending," said Estine.

"Yes all ended well," said Cora, but Ivy and Poppy were watching Edgar's face and were not so sure.

"And who did Meadowsweet choose?" asked Elzamere.

Edgar Lost and Found

"The wedding took place in April. I remember it was a beautiful day and Meadowsweet looked lovely. She had pink blossom in her pink hair and white blossom on her dress. Jasmine, Lupine and little Rosebud were her bridesmaids, and there were several best men, as is usual for a gnome wedding. I was one and so was Guffrey - so now you must have guessed - it was not I, nor Guffrey that she chose, but Robin.

When I first heard that they were to be wed, I felt resentment. I think Guffrey felt it too. Then I felt a sadness, as though there was one big empty space and I was sitting in it, and yet, I knew that Robin was a gentle soul who deserved happiness. Both Guffrey and I put on a brave face, we wished them well, and joined the wedding party.

Sometime later, I left Peddlecreek, and just like Jasper, I was searching for myself. After many years, I came to the South Downs. I found the ancient oak and made myself a new home."

For some moments, no one spoke, and then Elzamere asked. "And do you still feel that emptiness?"

"No indeed," he said, "I don't. You are my family now - and," said Edgar looking up, "I think, come the spring we should all take a trip to the West Country, to meet my friends, my very worthy friends in Peddlecreek."

And the fairies could think of nothing better.

Printed in Great Britain
by Amazon.co.uk, Ltd.,
Marston Gate.